Enticed by Desire

APRIL CROSS

DRAKE STORM

TWISTED ROSE
· PUBLISHING ·

CHAPTER 1

Eve

My phone won't stop buzzing. I grab it off the nightstand, glaring at the screen. Todd. Again.

"Fuck off," I mutter, tossing it back down. The phone skitters across the polished wood surface, screen flashing with his unread message.

I flop onto my back, staring at the faded glow-in-the-dark stars stuck to my ceiling since middle school. Growing up, I always dreamed I'd be engaged by age twenty-four to some fabulously wealthy older guy and planning my Caribbean cruise honeymoon. But here I am, single and living with my parents after graduating from college. I'm a loser. I've only had one boyfriend—Todd.

It's been two weeks since I caught Todd with my roommate. Two weeks of replaying his words: "You don't like sex." The accusation burns, settling into my chest like a stone.

I run my fingers through my hair, tugging slightly at the roots. My best friend, Andrea, is working tonight, and I'm left with nothing but the company of my own thoughts. Dangerous territory.

"This is pathetic," I say to the empty room.

Despite my efforts, the memory crashes through my mental defenses:

The weekend after graduation. Rhythmic creaking from down the hall. Pushing open the door to find Todd, naked and panting, between my room-mate's legs.

Her wide eyes spotting me first.

His face twisting with shock, then guilt. "Eve! I...it's not...You don't like sex..."

Ugh! I press my palms against my eyes, trying to physically block the image. Was he right? We never had actual sex because I never felt that spark with him. Does that make me broken somehow?

Fuck. What if I'm frigid?

A twenty-four-year-old virgin. Not entirely inexperienced—I've given blowjobs, enjoyed the power I felt sucking his cock and watching Todd come undone. But he never reciprocated, never went down on me. I can only imagine what a tongue would feel like.

To prove I can get turned on, I slide a hand between my legs and rub my pussy through my pajamas. As I stroke slowly up and down my mound, images of my parent's hot, older neighbor fill my mind. He's obviously off-limits, but I've always been drawn to older men. Their confidence, their experience...it's intoxicating. Maybe that was the problem with Todd—he was just a boy pretending to be a man.

My neighbor is Andrea's uncle Jasper, and my insides quiver as my fingertips glide up and down my cleft. My pajamas are getting damp, and I need more friction. I close my eyes, slipping my hand inside my panties. I sink a finger into my wet heat, fucking myself slowly. The sharp image of my neighbor morphs, becoming a faceless presence. Someone with broad shoulders and a trim waist, firm thighs...a man who knows how to make me come.

Whimpering, I remember when Andrea mentioned her uncle has a kinky lifestyle. She told me he dominates submissive women —whatever that means. I had to do some research online. All the BDSM websites I found made it sound amazing, and I'd often end up just as I was now, fingering myself as I wondered what it would be like to be a sub to an older hot dom. By the descriptions, the subs seemed to be just playthings for the dominant's pleasure. Did that feel good? To just be used by a big, strong man who can toss them around like a doll?

I didn't want to fuck Todd, so why would I want someone to just use me like that? But the daydream never fails to turn me into a needy mess. In my fantasy, the mystery man ties my hands, his touch gentle but unyielding as he fucks me slowly until I'm writhing in pleasure.

Mmm, okay, maybe letting someone use me like a sex doll wouldn't be so bad after all. Andrea's uncle supposedly has a dungeon in his basement, and I'd love to see whatever happens down there. I could give a guy complete control for a night and let him do whatever he wants to me. A throb of desire pulses between my legs, and right when I'm about to come, my cell phone lights up and rattles on my nightstand.

Motherfucker! I groan in frustration. I was soooo close. This better not be Todd again. I'd told him to stop contacting me two weeks ago but he keeps trying.

It's Andrea, thank God. I try to hide my heavy breathing when I answer. "Hey, why aren't you at work?"

Her silvery laugh rings out. "I *am* working, but I'm on a break. You won't believe what's going on."

Andrea's been my best friend since grade school, and I can tell she's got juicy gossip for me. I sit up, wiping my wet fingers on the edge of my shirt. "Ooooh, tell me!" My arousal fades, replaced by a burning curiosity.

"So, you know how I'm working for my uncle, right?"

I pick at a stray thread at the bottom of my shirt and watch in dismay as it unravels the seam a little. "Uh-huh."

Jasper hired her to help with his interior decorating company, which includes working some evenings.

"Yeah, so he's paying me to help at a kink party at his house tonight instead of my normal job."

Holy shit. My pussy clenches, and I immediately wonder what's happening at the party. What I wouldn't give to be a fly on the wall. Images flash through my mind—leather, chains, whips. Along with the sounds of people moaning in pleasure and pain.

Andrea drops to a conspiratorial whisper through the phone. "I've seen some crazy stuff. There's a line of women waiting to be tied up on a spanking bench. There're people fucking in front of everyone."

"Wow, sounds hot." Damn, I want to be at that party, but just to watch. What the fuck is a spanking bench? Wait, could Andrea get me in? My inexperience suddenly feels like a gaping hole in my life journey.

"It is," Andrea sighs. "But if my parents find out I'm working this party for my uncle, my life is over."

Holy hell, Andrea's parents would absolutely flip their lids if they knew. Andrea's always been the good girl—she volunteers at the animal shelter, sticks meticulously to her study schedule, and makes her bed every morning before breakfast, even while we were in college. Meanwhile, I'm basically her polar opposite. Sure, I might have left some of my wildest antics back in high school—like the time I got detention for ditching English class to go to a concert, or when I nearly got arrested for shoplifting lip gloss as a stupid dare—but even through college, trouble and I had stayed cozy friends. I'd argued my way into two meetings with my academic advisor my senior year, and I skipped lectures if something more interesting came up. Andrea might try to keep me in line, but honestly, I'm usually the one tempting her to let

4

loose a little, dragging her into adventures she'd never dare on her own.

"Yeah, my parents would flip too," I say, already plotting exactly how I might sneak over to Jasper's and peek through the windows. After all, a little trespassing never stopped me before—and it certainly won't tonight.

Andrea suddenly sounds perky. "Hey, so I called for a reason. I sort of forgot to get some ice. Can you run to the corner store and buy some? You can just leave them at the back door. Text me when they're there. It's better if you don't come in."

Wait, does she really think I'm not going to stick around to see what's going on? My heart races. This is my chance. "Sure. Give me a few, I'm in my pajamas. I'll try to be quick."

"Thanks, Eve."

After hanging up, I jump off the bed, energized. I'm going to that party, even if I have to sneak in. This is my opportunity to satisfy my curiosity.

Hmm, what exactly does one wear to a kink party? I mentally sift through all the research sites I've browsed in my efforts to understand BDSM. Digging through my closet, I select my tightest, shortest black skirt, fishnet stockings leftover from an old Halloween costume, and a black lace bra. My hands tremble slightly as I arrange everything on the bed. Something still feels missing—maybe a necklace?

Inspiration strikes as I remember the images on the websites. Fuck yeah, I'll wear our dog's old collar—there were tons of pictures of women wearing them. That'll look authentic.

Buster's collar and chain leash still hang on a peg by the back door, untouched since he passed. My parents kept them there as a way to remember him. A pang of guilt tugs at me as I lift them down—this probably isn't how they intended anyone to use them. Still, I can't help but think Buster, always playful and a little rebellious himself, would understand. And thankfully, he was a big, lovable boxer, which means the collar fits perfectly around my neck. After finishing my outfit, I add black eyeliner and bold red lipstick to complete the look. Damn, not bad. Oh shit, shoes. Quickly, I slide on my combat boots, fasten the collar into place, and study my reflection. Oh yeah—I definitely look badass.

Before I head out, I throw on my coat and zip it up all the way to hide the lacy bra and the collar. I'll ditch it when I get to the party. Texting Andrea that I'm on my way, I head toward my car in the driveway, keys in hand. Then I remember—the gas light had been blinking at me the last time I drove it. Damn it. I need to fill up first thing.

I glance at the time on my phone and sigh. The convenience store is only a few blocks away. Taking the car will waste time, and I'm already taking too long.

Screw it. I hurry to the garage and grab my bike instead. This will be way faster.

Two minutes and twenty-seven skirt adjustments later, I realize I've made a terrible miscalculation. What should have been a quick ride has turned into some bizarre stop-motion journey where I pedal three times, then stop to yank my skirt down before it becomes a belt.

"I'm a real genius," I grumble to myself, barely avoiding flashing an elderly man walking his dog. I turned a five-minute trip into the world's slowest peep show.

I have to keep one hand ready to tug the hem down when cars pass, which means I'm essentially riding one-handed at a snail's pace. At this rate, I could've driven to the gas station, filled up, gotten an oil change, and had the car detailed.

Definitely not my smartest wardrobe choice for cycling, but whatever. The party will be worth it—assuming I actually make it there before it ends.

I finally make it to the store, and trying to be as inconspicuous as possible, I stroll in casually. I'm just a woman buying ice —nothing to see here. After paying and another painstakingly slow ride back with the icy plastic bags hanging from my handlebars, I stash my bike beside her uncle's garage. My parents live in a wealthy neighborhood, so Jasper's house is enormous. It doesn't look like there's a party happening—but that would make sense if they're all in some dungeon setup in the basement. I sneak around to the back door, drop the bags on the ground, and try the handle.

Hell yeah, it's unlocked.

CHAPTER 2

Derek

"How much longer is this gonna take?" I ask my mechanics as they huddle under the car's hood in the last bay of my auto shop. "Maybe I should just call the guy? We can get it done in the morning."

"We got this," my second in command, Carl, tells me. He's ten years younger than me but has been underneath hoods and fenders since elementary school. "Let me lock up. We're just waiting for parts, I can handle it."

I grunt and squint at him. "You know how to complete the P.O.S. shit?" I ask, referring to our dated point-of-sale software, which can be tricky. "You know what to do if the card reader fucks up again?"

"Yeah, boss," he says, wiping his hand on a rag while the two mechanics discuss the repair, pointing at different places under the hood. "I've shadowed you for six months, man. I've earned the right to a key. I've got this. Don't you have some shindig tonight?"

Fuck, the party. I check my watch, and it's late enough that I won't have time to clean up much before I hightail it to Jasper's.

My escorts for the night are an old friend, Vanessa, and her new submissive. I agreed to mentor, coach, and act as a safety observer for their first impact play. I inhale a deep breath, then side-eye Carl. He's right—he can handle it. I'm just a control freak and can't let things go.

"Don't fuck this up," I growl, and unclip my shop keys and slam them in his palm. I grip his hand tight until he meets my eyes. "I'll cut your set of keys tomorrow."

His expression brightens but he keeps a straight face. "Don't worry about a thing, boss."

Giving him a short nod, I turn around and walk out the door. A lot of my persona here is different from how I behave away from work. The reason I use a firm hand with my mechanics is because there is a fine line between having fun while we service the automobiles and being sloppy and doing a poor job. I don't want a lawsuit from a customer getting killed because my guys were playing grab-ass on the shop floor and didn't secure a fucking brake line.

Scolding myself as I walk to my car, I realize I've gotta let go of the things I can't control. I've trained Carl since I hired him. Of all the grease monkeys in my employ, he has the most knowledge and experience under the hood. He's an excellent floor supervisor and he's ready to take more responsibility behind the counter and working with customers. My jaw relaxes when I push the tension out of my body and I slide behind the wheel of my 1994 Mustang GT, start it, and let the engine rumble at idle for a minute.

I close my eyes, and a vision of Jenny, my ex-girlfriend, appears. She's a fucking dime. Full rack, plump lips, blonde hair for miles. She could switch between playing good girl or tormenting me by being a teasing brat when we used to play at the kink parties Jasper throws. We got along incredibly well physically, but she wasn't satisfied with just my collar. She wanted more from me, specifically, she wanted me to put a ring on her finger. I couldn't do that. I wasn't the type of guy to lock a girl down to play house in the suburbs. She was wild when we were alone and in bed, but it never felt right to stick around after we finished.

I blink and push visions of my ex out of my mind to concentrate on the task at hand—being a dungeon monitor of sorts for Vanessa. I'd been in the kink scene in town since I moved here after graduation. The hometown of my best friend, Cole. I followed him here from our alma mater. No fucking way was I going to stay in my hometown. My dad was a vicious drunk, and my mom's moralistic judgement always rubbed me the wrong way. I live my life by my rules now, not theirs. The further away I got from both of them, the better. Cole's parents are cool and semi-adopted me midway through college, so coming home with him felt right.

I flip my arm behind the headrest of the passenger seat and back out, glancing out the rear window as I take my foot off the brake and slowly reverse to back out of my parking spot. My ride complains with a rumble wanting to roar out of the parking lot. But I keep her steady, breaking, shifting into drive, then cruising onto the road. It wouldn't be smart to be reckless in this part of town with all the traffic and cops. I can't have any delays on my way to Jasper's party. I have just enough time to make it home and change out of this corporate monkey suit and into something more appropriate.

I met Vanessa when she attended an introductory munch—a casual meeting of people in the BDSM lifestyle or interested in learning. Since then we've played regularly, and I basically trained her as a sub before she decided she enjoyed both topping and bottoming. Cole and I run in the same circles, still ten years after graduation. Jasper, who formed the hub of the small kink community here, is Cole's next-door neighbor. I remember when I met him for the first time. He waved me into his house to show me the dungeon he was building in his basement. We ended up pitching in with the construction, and Jasper mentored us as we learned our way around BDSM practices.

I close my eyes to enjoy a second of peace after parking in my driveway. Then I hurry inside and pull off my business owner outfit of a logoed white button-down shirt and chinos. I take a quick shower—pits and bits—since I'm on the sidelines tonight. Jenny doesn't come to the parties anymore.

Fuck. She's probably avoiding me.

I slick my hair back with some product, then pull on a sleeveless leather vest and faded jeans. After pulling on socks and work boots, I check the bathroom mirror, winking at myself confidently. I could meet Jenny 2.0 tonight, after all. I doubt it, but fuck, it's been too long already. I huff out a breath of frustration as I cruise out the door and hop back in my car. A twist of my key, she roars to life, and I reverse, then peel out, hauling ass down the quiet street.

I promised to be at Jasper's before Vanessa and her sub arrived so I could check out their dynamic, so I put the hammer down and swing through this quieter part of town, avoiding the busier streets with traffic and cops. I roll to a stop beside his house, climb out, and lock the door behind me. The night has a chill, but my leather vest is enough. I know I'll be plenty warm once things get rolling in the basement, even if my prospects of getting laid are low.

Jasper is outside on his porch talking to a couple, so I tip my chin at him as I pass by him and go inside. He knows why I'm here, and I'll let him handle the hosting and greet any first-timers. I grab two bottles of water from the half-filled cooler, skipping the cans of soda. I don't know who he put in charge of refreshments, but there are no energy drinks, and they're running low on ice. After downing one bottle, I toss it in the trash can and scan the faces of the people in the living room. The first floor is more for meeting and greeting people before pairing up and heading down to the dungeon. When I see

Vanessa, I lift my hand to get her attention, then start weaving through the crowd.

I check out her sub. She's a short blonde with nice tits, wearing a pair of cut-off shorts and a faded band T-shirt with razor rips between her breasts—not a bad get up for a first-timer. She's got a leather training collar snug around her neck; it's soft and padded, meant for play, not fashion. The same goes for the black cuffs already fastened to her wrists and ankles. I can tell she's nervous when she glances at me as I approach them, before returning her attention to Vanessa.

"Derek," I say, offering my hand. I don't recall her name, so I hope Vanessa will bail me out.

"This is Cammie," Vanessa says. Bingo—but I'm not going to bother to remember her name after this anyway. The cutie gazes at me with wide blue eyes that soften as she grins shyly. I lift her hand by the fingers and kiss across her knuckles, winking at Vanessa.

"I thought it might be good to talk first." Vanessa's nervous, too, but projecting enough confidence her sub can't see it.

"That's always a good idea." I usher them toward a sofa with two open cushions. I follow behind them, and Vanessa sinks into the end seat, then tugs her sub into her lap. She's shocked at first when Vanessa curls her fingers under the bottom of the collar and pulls her back against her body, but quickly relaxes as her domme's arms wrap around her.

"It's smart to talk things through," I say, giving both of them a comforting smile as I plop down on the opposite side of the couch. "Vanessa says this is your first time at a play party?"

Training new players is sensitive, with a mix of emotions and feelings wrapped in intense sensual situations. While these aren't my responsibility, I must be aware of them. My job is to help them learn safely. Role, impact, and rope play all involve some danger, and can be life-threatening if not monitored closely.

"She's never been spanked," Vanessa says, ignoring my question to her sub. Her hand runs along the girl's side. Cammie leans into her domme, nuzzling under her jaw before turning back to me and maintaining eye contact as her cheeks heat up from her domme's intimate touches.

"Never?" I ask. She shakes her head and nibbles on her lower lip. "Okay, are you interested in the sensation? Being swatted on your ass?"

She gives me a silent bob of her head. I smile and wink. "Use your words, sweetheart. You are an active participant in the role-play, and your voice is important."

She sighs then with a determined expression, she says, "I want to know what a spanking feels like." She slaps her hands together and makes a loud smack. "That hard on my butt."

I chuckle and glance past her at Vanessa. "You know her safeword?"

Cammie straightens, then peers over her shoulder at me. "Shortcake," she says before turning back to Vanessa. "That was my favorite doll growing up, Strawberry Shortcake."

"Okay, that's good." I smile, then address Vanessa. "Just your hand, or will you use a paddle or a cane?"

Vanessa lifts a shoulder and tilts her head. "I may use a paddle. We'll have to see how it goes."

"Touching?" I ask, raising one eyebrow.

"Yes, please," Cammie says to me, before returning her attention to her domme. "If it pleases you, Mistress."

So they've been working on their protocol, and the sub doesn't seem to be coerced. "Okay, I think we can move downstairs." I stand and hold my hand out to Cammie, who takes it and rises. Her body shivers with nervous energy as she walks toward the stairs. Vanessa pauses beside me as she smiles wickedly.

"I want her in tears," Vanessa whispers in my ear. "Real fucking tears, Derek."

She continues past me and I follow the pair down the narrow

stairs to Jasper's dungeon basement. This should be interesting. Vanessa's kink is topping, but she doesn't yet feel confident to command the scene, so I'm the dom by proxy. I anticipate the play session as energy coils in my core. Surveying the players already in the dungeon I notice plenty of sexy women, but I'm not attracted to any of them as they loiter in clumps watching the demonstrations. Sighing, I push my fingers through my hair. I'll be home alone by the end of the night.

CHAPTER 3
Eve

I sneak inside Jasper's house, my heart slamming against my ribs like it's trying to break free. Sweat slicks my palms as I frantically scan the dimly lit entryway for somewhere to hide. Spotting an open coat closet, I dart inside, squeezing between heavy coats that carry the musty, rich scent of aged leather. I leave the closet door cracked just enough to peer out, my breath catching as I glimpse shadowy shapes moving down the hallway, soft light filtering across glimpses of polished hardwood flooring and elegant furnishings.

My mind flashes back to my childhood, sneaking downstairs well after my bedtime to catch a glimpse of my parents' dinner parties. The thrill of the forbidden was intoxicating then, but it pales in comparison to the excitement coursing through me now.

I text Andrea that the ice is at the back door and put my phone on silent, holding my breath as footsteps approach. Andrea's familiar figure hurries past. She's wearing all black and her hair is pulled into a high ponytail. She usually wears light floral colors. This must be her trying to look professional.

As soon as she disappears through a nearby door with the ice,

I count to one hundred in my head, each second stretching like an eternity.

Just as I'm about to emerge, I hear more people nearby. I freeze, my heart in my throat as a guy says, "Did you hear something?"

"Nope," a woman responds. "Come on, you promised to show me your rope techniques."

They move away, and I let out a shaky breath. Fuck, that was too close. Part of me screams to leave now, to run back to the safety of my boring, predictable life. But a stronger, more insistent side urges me forward, hungry for the unknown.

Finally, I emerge from my hiding spot, leaving my coat on the floor of the closet. My stomach is in knots as I tiptoe towards the door Andrea used. The handle turns silently, revealing a staircase descending into a reddish glow.

Every step groans under my feet, and I wince. When I finally reach the bottom, the narrow stairway opens into a large room, instantly overwhelming my senses.

There are people in various stages of undress, their skin gleaming under the warm lighting. Leather creaks and chains jingle under a steady undercurrent of whispers, punctuated by an occasional sharp crack of something impacting flesh, followed by a shriek dissolving into the background of moans. It's so different from the fumbling, awkward encounters of my limited experience that I feel like I've stepped into another world entirely.

I edge along the wall, trying to blend in as my gaze darts around the room. To my left, a woman is bound to a large wooden X, and a man traces intricate patterns over her skin with something that looks like a feather. Her whimpers of pleasure send a shiver rippling down my spine, triggering an answering throb deep inside me.

Across the room, the sound of rhythmic smacks draws my attention. A woman is bent over a padded bench, her wrists and ankles secured by leather cuffs clipped to the base. Another woman stands behind her, wielding a paddle with practiced ease. Each impact makes the bound girl moan, and her skin flushes a beautiful pink.

A longing pulls at me as my panties dampen. What would that feel like?

I'm riveted to the spot, mesmerized and unable to look away. A woman in front of me shifts to the side and I move forward to stand next to her. I want a front-row view of this.

I'm so engrossed in the scene that I don't notice the man standing near the spanking bench until he speaks. "Harder. She can take it." His bark is clear and commanding

The woman with the paddle nods, adjusting her stance. The bound woman's next moan is louder, a mix of pain and ecstasy that makes my knees weak.

My breath catches as I look at the guy directing the action. He stands with his back to me, but even from this angle, I can see the power in his stance. Broad shoulders taper down to a narrow waist, muscles shifting under tanned skin as he moves. When he turns, scanning the crowd, I feel like I've been struck by lightning.

Mmm, he's yummy. He looks to be in his mid-thirties, and he's wearing nothing but a pair of jeans and shoes. His bare chest is broad and sculpted, and his well-defined arm muscles tell me he works out. Damn, this dude is fine. Wait...Why does he look so familiar?

OH...MY...FUCKING...GOD...It's Derek, my brother's best friend from college.

Our eyes lock, and for a moment, the rest of the room fades away. His gaze is intense, almost predatory. I'm rooted to the spot, and my core tightens when his eyes roam down my body. A blush creeps up my face as my nipples tighten. When he notices my collar, I fight the urge to fiddle with it.

Shit, does he remember me? Last time I saw him, I was still in high school. My mom had a surprise pregnancy late in life, making me much younger than my brother and his friends.

I do the math quickly in my head; that makes Derek about thirty-six. Now, he's...oh, god, he's magnificent.

My stomach somersaults, and a bead of sweat forms on my forehead. I'm so busted if he recognizes me, and I can't tell if he does. This uncertainty ramps up my anxiety. Shit, should I leave? I'm about to slip to the back of the crowd, but I pause and force myself to relax.

I can do this. What are the odds that he remembers me after all these years? I put on a fake smile and nod casually at him.

When the woman being paddled cries out again in a high-pitched wail, he tears his eyes away and addresses the two women. "Stop, she's had enough."

The velvety timbre of his command echoes in my head and an unfamiliar yearning spreads through my veins. Holy fuck, he owns this space and these women with his commands. Is this the thrill of BDSM and why people do it?

When Derek caresses one of the women's shoulders, a spark of arousal surges through me overlaid with jealousy. I want his hands on me.

Wait, what the fuck? I've never felt this way before—not when Todd touched me or even looked at me. The thought of being within arm's reach of my brother's best friend is enough to make me tingle with desire.

He unclips the woman on the bench and helps her stand. Hmm, I wonder what it would be like to have him dominate me. Would he tie me up and use me however he wants, and would he make sure I got off too? I really shouldn't be thinking about him this way, but I can't help myself.

Seeing and hearing everything is messing with my head. Here I am, aching to know what it feels like to be spanked and bound before I've even had sex. But maybe there's nothing wrong with me at all—maybe this is exactly what I've needed all along, someone who can take control and show me what I've been missing.

Derek leads the woman to an empty couch, steadying her as she stumbles. When he tenderly wipes a stray tear from her cheek, a bittersweet warmth fills me. Damn it, I want to be her.

She leans into him for support and he whispers something in her ear before kissing her forehead and stepping away. Huh, what did he say to her?

The woman using the paddle returns, sitting beside the girl she was just spanking and pulling her into her lap. They share an intense look as they cuddle, the spanker softly caressing the spankee—ooh, that's sweet. Derek returns with bottles of water, handing them to the women while they make room for him beside them. He sits down, rubbing the bare arm of the girl sitting on the other's lap, then his eyes meet mine again.

Electricity ripples down my back, and my nipples stiffen painfully again. I was so focused on them, I didn't notice the crowd had wandered away. I'm the only one left watching, standing alone in the middle of the room.

A current of lust burns through me as he gives me an impish smile. When he winks, my stomach flips. Fuck, I think he recognizes me.

I'm so screwed. And god help me, I think I want to be.

CHAPTER 4
Derek

I relax on the couch beside the tired pair, cuddling together, gazing sweetly at each other. I stopped the scene because—shit, what's her name?—Cammie was exhibiting signs of distress and I wasn't confident she'd remember to use her safe word. I played with Vanessa before she decided she was more of a switch and wanted to practice topping. She occasionally asks me to play with her and her dates at parties like this. Vanessa gets off on being told what to do to her sub as though she doesn't want to spank her submissive, she's just doing what she's told. I smirk at the mind game she plays with herself.

They seem to be settling down, holding eye contact, kissing softly. Their soft whispers are none of my business, and I feel very detached from their intimacy. Since I don't have a sub of my own right now, assuming the trainer role works for me. I get to see the light in their eyes when they get it, but it's not the same as seeing my sub respond.

I pan across the room, noticing the sexy young woman still standing in the middle of the room, even though the show is over. There's something familiar about her, but I haven't seen her at one of Jasper's parties before. She's fucking sex on a stick, the little clothes she's wearing are all black and the collar around her neck adds to the odd goth style she's rocking. She's younger than Cammie, which makes her way too young for me. But an itch inside me wants to stride across the room, take her in my arms, and whisper naughty things in her ear. I give her a wicked smile and wink, even if I'm not the only guy staring at her.

She fidgets, rubbing her thighs together as she looks back at Vanessa and her sub. It's hot as hell that she's turned on by watching the pair. I reckon it's her first time at a kink party with how skittish she appears, but it's not unusual for some subs to get so aroused they need a little relief. Her dom will probably come to claim her soon and take her into one of the private rooms in the dungeon and play with her and some of the toys available. But she's been alone for a while—where the fuck is her dom?

Jasper appears beside me and claps a hand on my shoulder. "Hey guys, nice show."

Vanessa smiles at him, and I laugh. "Thanks, Jas."

He turns to me. "Where's Jenny?"

I shrug. "She got bored with me."

I don't add that what Jenny got tired of was waiting for me to propose.

He pauses for a moment then continues in his deep baritone, "Well, you won't have any trouble finding someone else."

It's true—women practically throw themselves at me. "Nah, probably not."

I tilt my head toward the gorgeous chick still standing nearby. "Who does she belong to?"

Fuck, why am I asking about her? She's too young for me, and she's fucking collared. But she's wearing a tiny skirt that barely covers the tops of her shapely fishnet covered thighs. I can almost tell the color of her panties. She's only wearing a black lace bra, sheer enough for me to wonder about the color of her nipples. Her eyes are made up with dark eyeliner and mascara which make her bright red lipstick pop.

Jasper glances at her and then does a double take before growling, "Fuck, she's friends with Andrea. But I know she wasn't invited."

"Andrea, huh?" I don't know who that is, but if she's here with another woman, that explains why the girl seemed turned on by Vanessa and her sub.

Jasper whistles a sharp pattern, and the girl turns her attention to him like she recognizes the tune. Her eyes widen, dart to me, then snap back to Jasper, appearing spooked.

Jasper grunts. "Eh, fuck. I got no idea why Evelyn's here. I'll need to talk to Andrea about not inviting strays."

Evelyn. Pretty name. But wait, why isn't she allowed to be here? And stray? She's wearing a collar. For fuck's sake. Where's her fucking dom?

Before I can ask, Jasper strides over to her. I can't hear what he says, but I can tell he's scolding her from across the room. She stands apologetically with downcast eyes, staring at her combat boots. My cock comes to life watching her response to Jasper's gruff lecture.

My mind takes a detour as I fantasize about her on her knees in front of me with her mouth open. My cock twitches at the thought. Shit, I gotta get laid soon. I break off from watching them talk because I shouldn't get worked up about some college chick.

After a few minutes of talking, Evelyn leaves, hurrying up the steps as Jasper returns to me. He seems agitated. I'm curious about the woman, but I try not to sound too nosy. "Problems?"

"Her parents are going to be fucking pissed if they find out she was here. I don't need my neighbors thinking I'm corrupting their innocent daughter."

I'm about to tell him she's collared so she can't be that innocent, when the realization hits me like a bucket of ice water.

Neighbors? My best friend Cole grew up next door, and his parents still live there. That's his little sister—Evie? Oh shit, I'm going to hell—and Cole will help me get there faster if he ever finds out I was fantasizing about fucking his sister's throat.

I play it cool, acting distracted. "Yeah, but I doubt she'll tell her parents she was here."

He snorts. "That's true."

When Jasper pans around the room, I can tell he's done with the conversation, and I'm relieved. I need to clear my mind of any indecent thoughts about Evie. It's been years since I saw her. She had always been cute in a bratty way. She hated Cole's nickname for her and scowled whenever he called her Evie. I never would've guessed she'd turn into such a sultry, sexy woman. And a BDSM submissive, too. My cock throbs.

Yeah, I'm going straight to the bad hell.

Jasper nudges me with his elbow. "Hey man, I'm going to go have a little chat with Andrea."

I bob my head, ready to leave. "I'm heading out. I'll talk to you later."

"Thanks for coming," He smiles before disappearing up the stairs.

When he leaves, I scan the room one last time. I don't see anyone interesting, but I can't help but wonder if Evie might reappear. When she doesn't, disappointment washes over me, but I let it go. Seeing Cole will be difficult if I keep thinking about his little sister, all grown up and wearing a collar. I cut off that thought before it goes too far, but I'm irritated that she was alone. Who is her dom? If she keeps showing up at Jasper's parties, my life will get more complicated.

What if her brother had come to the party tonight? He sometimes does. Hell, he might know what Evie's into. I doubt he'd tell me she's someone's submissive, but a little heads up that she might be at Jasper's party would've been nice if he'd known.

I say my goodbyes to Vanessa and her sub and grab my vest

from where I left it near the spanking bench. The basement has a separate exit, so I slip out without running into anyone. It's colder than it was when I got here, which is good since I got overheated thinking about Evie's mouth. I watch Cole's childhood home as I get into my car. Lights are on in one of the upstairs bedrooms— probably her room. If she's grown up to be an adult brat, someone will have their hands full with her. I start my car and think about how her breasts would be more than a handful.

Fuck, I gotta get a grip.

CHAPTER 5
Derek

Wh…hen I get back, my house is quiet—too fucking quiet. I prefer being alone, but tonight, I need something to distract me from Eve's luscious curves that dance around in my mind. What if I brought her home with me? I could press her against the wall, pin her wrists above her head, kiss her, and….

Fuck! Stop it. She's off-limits with an all-caps OFF.

I change into my pajama pants and snag a bag of chips and turn on the TV. Flipping through channels, I settle on watching a wrestling match. The noise from the show fills the air. Eh, it'll do.

I manage to distract myself for five whole minutes before my thoughts drift to Evie—specifically, her mouth. Even from a distance, I could tell her lips were full and tempting. I'd like to grip that collar and pull her down to my cock, watch as she smears the bright red lipstick she wore along my shaft as if she were claiming me. Mmmm, the things I'd do to that mouth...

Goddammit. Jesus, I need to get her out of my head. For fuck's sake, I shouldn't be fantasizing about her like this.

I've never been this affected by just watching a woman before. It must be the lack of sex since Jenny, making me feral.

But what's the harm in a bit of fantasy? I'd never touch Eve in a million years—my best friend's little sister is verboten—unless she begged.

I shake my head to clear it. It's hard to believe Evie's grown up into a sexy little submissive. She must be in her mid-twenties. Damn, I'm getting old. I probably should have proposed to Jenny. Then I'd be snuggled up with her tonight instead of drooling over the taboo fantasy of Evie's red lips wrapped around my cock.

When an infomercial for non-stick pans starts playing, I realize I haven't paid attention to wrestling. Instead, I'm stroking my cock through my pants and replaying the spanking scene from the party in my head. Except it's Evie's ass getting paddled, and her throaty cries from the impact intermixed with whimpers of pleasure.

Closing my eyes, I let the fantasy grow, thinking of Evie strapped to the bench with just a ribbon of lace snug between her cheeks pulled tight against her sex.

I'd gently run my fingers over her ass and then slap it, using a lighter hand with her to start. Then I'd give a few soft slaps to warm her up before building slowly into a firm spanking.

I groan as my cock throbs at the thought, and I imagine the feel of her ass warming under my fingers. I push one hand inside my waistband and grip my dick, jerking and speeding up the tempo of my stroking while the fantasy unreels in my mind.

Eve squirms under my touch as I increase the force of each strike. She trembles from the impact—every smack sending shivers of pain intermixed with pleasure rushing through her. She cries, pleads, and whines, shifting her body on the bench as I continue. Her skin's covered with sweat, and her hair is plastered against her cheek as she glances over her shoulder. Tracing my fingers over her heated ass, I pull the sliver of her thong to the side, finding her dripping wet. That's when she finally breaks, desperate for release, begging me to touch her, finger her. Make her come.

Oh no, she's not coming until I'm inside her.

After untying and carrying her to the bed, I toss her on her back and crawl beside her. I grip her thighs, spreading her open as I stare down at her. Watching her expression as I tease her with the tip of my cock. Listening to her whimper as I draw my tip along her glistening slit. I'm going to fuck her until she's hoarse from screaming my name.

I stroke myself harder, past the point of holding back, then moan in frustration as I can practically feel her warmth and wetness surrounding me.

I sink balls deep into her sweet pussy, blasting my cum as her velvet walls squeeze and milk me. Rippling around my shaft until I'm completely spent.

An insatiable hunger rises inside me. I know this is so fucking wrong, but I can't stop fantasizing about her. I want something impossible to have. When I picture her on all fours with me plowing into her from behind, it only takes a few more seconds of stroking before I explode. I moan loudly as my cum shoots onto my belly and spills down the side of my hand.

I curse at myself as the high wears off. Reality sets in as I grab some tissues and clean up the mess. Jesus Christ, it might be time to find a new girlfriend. Not only is Evie Cole's sister, but she's also someone's collared submissive. Jealousy floods through me at the thought, which is stupid. I don't know who the fuck they are, or why she was alone for much of the night. Maybe they're a great person who cares for her like a good dom should.

Mother fucker. They'd better.

Now that I've climaxed, I relax and flip through the TV show options, finding a stand-up comedian. A little laughter might help erase the memory of me getting off thinking about Evie. Thank god she's collared. I'm not sure I could stay away from her otherwise.

By the time the show finishes, I can't keep my eyes open.

Sunday is my usual day for running errands as the shop is closed. Since I need to get things done before the work week starts again, and Mondays are our busiest days, I finish as much as possible on the weekends.

My house is mostly clean, and I'm sitting at the kitchen table, picking at a plate of leftover spaghetti and going over my to-do list when my cell rings. Fuck, it's Cole. I mean, I'm happy to hear from him, but I'm still entertaining thoughts of Evie spread over the hood of my car with her ankles on my shoulders.

I swipe to answer and hold it up to my ear. "Hey, man. How's it going?"

Cole laughs. "You know, the usual, just living the dream."

I'm curious why he called, we talk every week, but usually only by text or email. Talking on the phone is tedious, and I hate it because I have to be polite with rude customers. Thankfully, he gets right to the point. "Hey, are you free for dinner next Saturday?"

I immediately feel suspicious—and guilty. Did Evie tell him she saw me last night?

Cole catches my hesitation. "Is this getting through? Fuck, man, answer my question. You do eat, right?"

I chuckle. "Okay, okay, sorry. I'm a little distracted. Yeah, sure. I can make it."

"Awesome. Listen, my parents are out of town cruising the Caribbean, and Evie's at the house alone," Cole says casually. "They asked me to check in on her a few times to make sure she hasn't burned the house down with her awful cooking. I thought I'd grill some steaks at the folks' place. Does seven o'clock work for you? I love my sister, but it'd be fucking boring just her and me. We could play Uno or some shit."

Goddamn, I can't back out now, I'd be an asshole after saying I could make it. If he'd told me from the start that Evie was part of the plan, I could have devised some bullshit excuse. Now I'm picturing sitting across from Evie and my mind drifts to her in a lacy bra with a collar before I catch myself. Goddamn, that will be fucking torture. But, hell—maybe it'll be a good thing. If we hang out, play cards, I'll remember she's just Cole's bratty little sister, not some tempting submissive. What the fuck, why not? "Sure, sounds great."

Cole is still chuckling, and I smile at his good humor. We say our goodbyes, and when I disconnect, I stare at my pasta. Fuck, now my appetite's gone. It's going to be a long week until Saturday.

CHAPTER 6

Eve

W hat a shitty start to my week. I'm supposed to be job
hunting—hence the sensible skirt, neat blouse, and
"please hire me" smile I practiced in the mirror this morning—
but instead, here I am, watching my car get towed like the
universe is giving me the middle finger. I figured I'd be responsible and grab groceries first. Big mistake. Steam poured out from
under the hood like I summoned a demon, and now my trusty
little car is getting hauled to the nearest mechanic. Yeah, this
can't be good.

Once my car is wheeled up on the flatbed, the tow truck
driver turns to me. "Miss, do you want a ride to the mechanic's
shop? It's a bit of a walk."

A bit of a walk? It's two blocks. Do I look like the princess
type who wouldn't want to walk...or is he just being nice and I'm
in a foul mood?

"Nah, thanks. I'm going to enjoy the fresh air on the way
there."

He gives me a kind smile. "Understood. Have a good day,
miss."

As he drives away, I take a deep breath and try to calm down. This is so not how I wanted to start my week. I'm glad he offered me a ride, but the walk will give me time to think. Plus, the weather is beautiful.

I pop my earbuds in and increase my pace, humming along to the music. This better not cost a fortune to fix. Asking my parents for money sucks, especially since I don't have a job. Maybe it won't hurt too much. I can swing a couple hundred bucks.

The auto repair shop appears ahead of me and there are several cars waiting outside, which is reassuring. A guy wearing oil-stained coveralls is walking around my car. A tall, brown-haired man in a white shirt and khakis walks out to greet another customer and I freeze.

Oh no way, it's Derek—he works here? Why didn't I know this? Should I try another shop?

As I turn to leave, Derek waves. Shit, he saw me. What're the odds? First I spot him at Jasper's party, and now he works at the mechanic's shop.

When he looks at me quizzically, I realize I'm still staring like a fool, so I wave back. Ugh, I'm acting like a total dork. An image of him at the party pops into my head and my body heats up. I'll just talk to him so I can leave quickly. I don't trust myself not to do or say something stupid around him.

As I walk toward him, he meets me halfway. Up close his eyes are gorgeous—a perfect mix of grassy green and emerald. Were they always this spectacular? He runs his gaze over me and I flush, fighting the urge to squirm.

When he holds out his hand, his voice is deep and smooth, just like I remembered, but now with a velvety undercurrent. "Little Evie, that you?"

I swallow, trying to get my mouth to work properly, and all I manage is, "Yep."

I hate my brother's nickname for me, but something in

Derek's tone keeps me from snarling back a correction. From him it's almost... nice. I'm already mentally kicking myself for being an idiot. Way to sound sexy, Eve. Derek grins and my stomach flutters as I shake his hand awkwardly. "Hi."

He arches an eyebrow like he's amused. "Are you okay?"

This isn't going well. "Sorry, I'm freaking out."

"Something happen?"

When I glance over at my still-steaming car, he follows my line of sight and understanding dawns on his face. "Ah, I take it that's yours?"

I try to explain. "It started spewing. Called roadside assistance and they towed it here."

"Let's go take a look."

My body buzzes from being so close to him, but I stay composed. I spend the next few minutes watching Derek under the hood and tinkering with various tools. Finally, he wipes his hands on a rag he pulls from his back pocket.

"You have a busted radiator hose. A few actually. My guys can fix it, but I have to call to see if we can get the parts."

When he names the price, I sigh in relief. It's not as bad as I expected. It'll drain my savings account, but I can manage it without asking my parents for help.

Derek calls over another employee, and they chat about my car while I sneak peeks at Derek. The other guy goes back inside the shop, and Derek turns to me. "The parts are available; we just need to wait for them to be delivered, then we can get to work. It'll be a couple of hours, is that okay?"

Shit. There goes my job-hunting plans for this afternoon, but I'm lucky they can fix it today.

Derek's still talking. "I can give you a lift somewhere, if you need a ride."

No way do I want to sit next to him in a small, enclosed space with how my body's reacting to him. "Nah, I'll call my friend."

"All right. The offer's there. Let's get the paperwork started."

I keep my expression neutral and follow him inside. Walking behind him, I can't help but notice the way his trousers cling to his ass—and what an absolutely perfect ass it is. Yep, I've definitely got the hots for him.

As I fill out the forms, I realize I've been staring at the same line for way too long—permission to operate vehicle. My brain, unhelpful as ever, drifts to thoughts of him operating me, and suddenly my handwriting goes a little crooked. This checklist isn't doing me any favors either. My eyes catch on the word lubricant and I rub my thighs together, like that'll stop the thoughts rushing in. I press the pen to the paper harder than necessary, trying to finish fast, but I keep imagining him tying me up and fucking me. I've got to get out of here.

When I'm finished, he takes them from me. "I'll give you a call when it's ready. Have a good afternoon, Eve."

"Thanks."

I force myself to turn and I walk outside, taking a few deep breaths of fresh air. This is messed up. He's older, and hot, but there's no way I can do anything with him. Not that I even know if he'd be interested, but my brother would freak—especially since what I want Derek to do to me isn't just sex.

I get a vision of me crawling toward him on the concrete floor of his shop, and I instantly try to erase it. Why do I keep thinking about kinky stuff around him? Shit, I'm crushing on him. When Todd cheated on me, I felt a sense of relief, so I don't trust my judgement in men. What is it about Derek that has me so attracted to him and wanting him to dominate and control me?

Wait...why can't he? Who's going to tell my brother? All this time I've been saving my virginity for someone who turns me on, and now I've found a guy who does and I'm not going to do anything about it?

Am I crazy? Oh, god. I think I'm losing it.

"Evie?"

I startle and spin around to find Derek staring down at me. Fuck, did I say any of that out loud? How long have I been standing here?

He tilts his head at me. His tone is concerned. "You sure you don't need a ride?"

What I need is for him to give me a command so I can see how it feels. I have a strange urge to make him see me as a desirable woman. It's time to try flirting.

I dip my head, looking at him through my eyelashes. "It depends on what kind of ride you're offering."

Derek blinks, then a grin slowly spreads across his face and his eyes twinkle. "Baby girl, there's only one kind of ride I'd be offering my best friend's sister." He waves at his classic Mustang GT. "Do you want me to take you home?"

I blush, unsure of what to do now that he didn't take the bait. "Sure."

Derek motions with his chin. "Follow me."

He stops by the open bay and calls in to tell the other guy he's taking me home. When we get to his car, he opens the passenger door for me, like a gentleman. "Your chariot awaits."

Once he's in the driver's seat, energy crackles along my skin and my mouth goes dry from being so close to him. All I can manage is a weak, "Thanks for this."

He flips on the radio as he merges onto the highway. The music fills the silence, but my brain still races the longer we sit without talking. Why doesn't he mention the party? Should I say something? Fuck it, I'm doing it.

"So...." I reach over and turn the volume down a notch. "About last night..."

"Yes? You looked lovely, by the way."

My stomach flips. Lovely? That's not what I expected him to say. My brain blips out. What were we talking about? Oh right. "Um, yeah, about that. Please don't tell my brother, okay?"

His eyebrows lift, just for a moment, before his expression smooths over and he concentrates on the road. "I wouldn't."

There's a beat of silence before he casually asks, "Did your dom bring you?"

My heart stutters. Shit. What the hell am I supposed to say to that?

CHAPTER 7

Eve

Derek waits for me to answer, and after a few moments of silence, he says, "Forget it, I shouldn't have asked."

I decide to be honest. "No, it's fine. I don't have one."

"You were wearing a collar."

I'm not going to admit it was an actual dog's collar, so I ignore his comment. "I was just watching. That's okay, right?"

"Yeah. There's nothing wrong with that. It was all I was doing, too. I was making sure everyone was safe."

Last night was interesting to watch, but I would have preferred it if Derek had been spanking me. Oh god, why do I keep thinking these things? Heat rushes to my face, and I fight the urge to fan myself with my hand. This is going to be a long drive if all I can think about is sexual scenarios involving him dominating me. A tingle between my legs makes me shift uncomfortably in the seat. "Sorry. It was my first time seeing something like...that."

Derek peeks over at me. "What did you think?"

This is such a weird conversation to be having with my brother's college friend... but I'm kind of into it. It's strange, in a good way. No one's ever actually asked me what I thought about sex before—not Todd, that's for sure. With him, it was always about what he wanted, never what I might've felt or been curious about. Derek hasn't even touched me and somehow he's already making me feel more seen. He keeps his eyes on the road, which makes it difficult to gauge how honest I should be. Still, the truth bubbles up before I can second-guess it. "It was hot as hell."

"You liked it, huh?" Derek sounds pleased, and that gives me the confidence to continue.

"Yeah, I did."

He grips the steering wheel tighter. "Spankings are hot."

I'm about to tell him about the BDSM websites I looked at, but then he speaks again. "So, no dom...Are you single?"

Holy shit, is he asking because he's interested in me? Butterflies dance in my stomach, and I sit up straighter, trying to fake some confidence. "Why? Do you want to go on a date and spank me?"

Derek laughs and reaches over, takes my hand in his, squeezing for a moment before letting go and returning it to the steering wheel. "Sorry baby girl. I'm way too old for you."

My skin feels branded from his touch, and I blush, staring down at my hand in my lap before sneaking a sideways glance at him. "Good point. You probably couldn't keep up."

Derek whistles. "Ouch. Remind me not to underestimate you."

The air shifts, a teasing spark still lingering between us before his tone turns a shade more serious. "I was just curious. Not everyone in the scene is...well, safe."

Now I'm even more interested in knowing what he meant, but I don't want to come right out and ask. Instead, I tease, "So... would you tie me up and use me if we went out?"

His head turns slightly, and a thrill runs through me when I see a flash of heat in his eyes. But he finally answers with a firm, "No."

He catches me off guard—not because I expected a yes, but because of how sure he sounds. I can't help myself. I poke at him again. "Why not? Isn't that what doms do?"

He doesn't answer right away. Just breathes in deep and lets it out slowly, like he's picking his words. "Eve, listen. If we ever hooked up—which is not happening—you wouldn't be just a toy for me to play with. This lifestyle means something to me, and I take it seriously."

A toy. That word sticks in my brain, clinging like static. It drowns out the rest for a second. A toy. Used, played with, discarded? Or something cherished?

Derek concentrates on the road, but his next words are softer. "You wouldn't be just a sex toy. That's not my style. Sex isn't what dominance and submission is about."

I snort before I can stop myself, then clap my hand over my mouth. "Sorry, but… what does that even mean? There were literally people fucking in that room."

He laughs quietly, the tension in his shoulders easing. "What I mean is I'd never treat you like an object. I wouldn't be selfish. As a dominant, the submissive's pleasure is important to me. More than my own. BDSM is like a partnership. Yin and yang."

His words sink in. That doesn't sound like just sex—it sounds like something more, like dating. A smile spreads across my face at the thought of being with Derek. "Really?"

He lets out a slow breath and glances over at me. Our eyes meet, and my heart races when something electric passes between us. "I worship my subs and take care of them. Power exchange is fucking hot, but it's not just about sex."

Worship? Damn, that sounds amazing. Todd was selfish and always focused on himself, so this kind of arrangement is totally unfamiliar to me. "So you're not into the rough stuff?"

"Baby girl, you have no idea what you're getting yourself into."

I almost say 'try me,' but I stop myself just in time. Why do I feel so bold suddenly? Maybe I can convince him to teach me a thing or two. "So, how does it work between a dom and sub?"

"We're not doing this, Evie."

Now I'm confused, and a little frustrated. "Doing what?"

"This. Us. Together. You need someone your age. Someone who didn't know you when you were fourteen, wearing braces."

I frown in irritation. What's the big deal? It's just sex. It doesn't have to be a whole thing with feelings and commitment. I should probably drop it, but the words come anyway. "I'm not asking for a commitment. People can fuck without dating, you know."

His posture shifts—tense, closed off. The easy air between us evaporates. When the car slows and he pulls off onto the shoulder, my stomach knots. Shit. Is he really that mad?

The car comes to a stop, and he lets the engine idle. My stomach clenches, and my pulse thuds in my ears. What is he doing? Is he going to kick me out here?

He says nothing for a long moment before breaking the silence. "You deserve to be with someone who actually gives a damn about you, Evie."

"Um, thanks, I guess." I cross my arms, heat rising to my cheeks. I hate it when people think they know what's best for me.

He exhales loudly. "This is going in circles. I don't even know how we got here."

I shift in my seat, suddenly aware of how far I pushed. "Okay," I say quietly. "I'm sorry." This is embarrassing.

There's a tightness in Derek's shoulders, like he's still unsettled. "Hey, it's fine."

He pulls back onto the road, and silence settles between us. I watch the scenery blur past, trying not to think about any of it.

When he clears his throat, the sound jolts me. "Listen, Eve." Suddenly I miss him calling me Evie. Eve is too formal coming from him. "Let's forget we saw each other at Jasper's."

Does he really think I'll just forget? Whatever.

"Fine," I mutter. "You never saw me, I never saw you."

The silence stretches again, this time heavier. After a beat, he speaks up. "Will you need a ride when your car is ready?"

So we're just going to pretend to be friendly? Got it. I can do that. "No thanks. I'll have Andrea take me."

Derek reaches over and turns the radio's volume up. That's my cue to shut up, I think, and look back out the window. Within a few minutes, he pulls into the driveway of my parents' house and doesn't cut the engine. I get the message, dude. I'll get out.

He doesn't look at me when he speaks. "Well, here you go. Have a good afternoon, Eve."

"Thanks." Why does my name sound so off when he says it like that? I much preferred it when he called me Evie.

I open the door and get out. When he doesn't drive off, I'm guessing he's waiting until I'm safely inside. As I unlock the front door, I glance back to find him still watching me so I give him a little wave.

Derek's car backs out of the driveway, and right before he drives off, he finally returns my wave.

I'm confused...and turned on. What is it about him that makes me want to do and say crazy things?

I step inside the house and as soon as the door closes behind me, my cell phone vibrates with a text message.

DEREK:

Call me if you want a ride to get your car.

I hug myself, squeal, and do a little happy dance. Did he pull over to text me? But...how did he have my number on his phone?

CHAPTER 8
Derek

When I return to the shop, I pull my phone out of my pocket. There's a text alert, so I unlock it with a swipe and glance at the screen. A text from Eve. She'd scribbled her number on the paperwork earlier. I've always had this weird thing with numbers—they stick in my mind instantly, like they're tattooed there. The moment I watched her pen move across the paper, her digits burned themselves into my brain.

EVE:

Yes, Daddy.

Daddy. The word rolls around in my head, hardening my cock. She thinks she's being funny, but she has no clue what the thought of hearing those words coming from her does to me. Jesus, I'm right back to envisioning her on her knees, mouth open and tongue out, gazing up at me with lust. Fuck, I don't want to be turned on by Evie, but hell. *Daddy*....

Growling under my breath in frustration at my lack of restraint when it comes to the vixen, I almost wish her car hadn't broken down near my garage. I mean, plenty of repair shops in town could have handled it.

47

My stomach tightens as I debate what to do about the text. I should respond and tell her to cut it out, but I blink at the words again. No, she might be trying to get me to answer. I'll leave it on read. She's just joking around and being a brat. She can't know how it affects me, and I can't let her get under my skin.

What if she's already there?

I shove that stray thought away and stalk through the shop floor, heading toward Joel, the mechanic assigned to Evie's car. He updates me about repairs he's doing, and I relax, welcoming the distraction. If I throw myself into work, maybe I'll stop thinking about how Cole's little sister practically told me she wants to fuck me with no strings attached. The fact that I'm tempted to take her up on it highlights my current lack of a submissive. I only commit myself to one woman at a time. I can't play the poly game. This stuff is ingrained in me, and I enjoy the singular attention of one partner. If I were with someone, Evie wouldn't affect me as easily. My lack of release is getting to me.

I distance myself from her car, telling Joel to prioritize it and instructing him to contact her when the repairs are finished. This way, I don't have to think about her or call her when the repairs are completed.

It doesn't work.

All afternoon, I'm distracted by the memory of her scent—orange with a hint of vanilla—her voice, and her teasing. This is fucking torture.

A few hours later, Joel finds me in the office. "Derek, the young woman's here to pick up her car. She's asking for you," he says knowingly.

"Shit," I groan. "Why does she want to talk to me?"

He shrugs. "Want me to tell her you're busy?"

I run my hand through my hair, wondering what Evie wants. "Nah, man. I'll take care of her."

I stop to enjoy the view as I enter the customer area, finding her leaning on the front desk and scrolling through her phone.

She's resting her elbows on the counter, holding the phone in both hands. She's changed clothes from before and is now wearing a snug T-shirt that displays way too much of her delicious tits. Her pair of jean shorts appear painted on, showing off her round ass and shapely legs. Holy fuck, she's got a tight little body. My cock twitches when she shifts her position, enticing me to examine her curves again. I smirk before coughing lightly. Did she change her clothes to try to impress me?

Her face lights up when she turns and spots me. "Hi."

Her happiness is contagious, and my irritation with her from earlier evaporates. "Hey, did you have a good day?"

"I didn't have to job hunt, so that was nice." She bounces on her heels like she's excited. She's fucking adorable.

I guess we've moved past our tiff in the car earlier, so I relax. But I can't help but glance at her mouth briefly before forcing myself to meet her eyes. Her beautiful brown irises—this isn't helping. "Did Joel ring you up and give you the car keys?"

Eve pats her purse. "Yeah, I'm good."

Then why does she want to talk to me? The air between us thickens with unspoken words and desires. Tension builds, and taking what she seems to be offering is so tempting. I could pull her into my office, press her against the wall, and show her how I worship my subs. I could have my hands all over her body, actually touching those curves I'm lusting over. Squeezing that round ass, pulling her hips into mine so she can feel what she's doing to me. I can almost hear her moan with desire....

Fuck. Stop it brain. I clear my throat and try to act like nothing is happening. "Well, let me know if you have any problems."

Eve bites her lip before sighing. "Yeah, okay. Bye."

I watch her leave, wondering why I feel like the biggest idiot in the world. This is ridiculous; I barely know her other than as Cole's little sister. After Saturday, I won't see her again and forget all about her. She's not the first chick I've found sexy, nor will she be the last. I know many women who would enjoy being the center of my attention. It's not a big deal for me to find a willing partner.

After a few days, I realize dismissing her from my fantasies is not easy. Every time my phone buzzes, I hope it's her. What is it about her that's got me so jumpy?

As Saturday evening approaches, I'm restless and agitated, with nothing to distract myself from thinking about her. It's been too long since I've had a woman in my bed, so I scroll through my contacts, considering who would be likely to agree to a hook-up without any drama.

While browsing familiar names, Evie's face pops into my mind as if she's looking over my shoulder. I groan and toss my phone onto the couch next to me. Jesus, why can't I stop thinking about her? It's like she's in my veins, and all I can think about is fucking her.

As if on cue, my phone vibrates. Shit, it better not be her. My defenses are getting weak. Maybe it's Cole. I lean over and glance at the screen, then roll my eyes. Of course, it's her.

EVE:

So are you coming to dinner on Saturday? Cole said he invited you.

Now is the perfect time to make up an excuse and cancel. I have no business being anywhere near her, smelling her perfume, feeling the heat of her body... Dammit. Spending the evening with her and Cole would be frustrating and torturous. Still, I'm too curious, wanting to learn more about her beyond fucking her senseless. What type of food does she like? What's her favorite color? What movies she enjoys. Does she read books? Does she like the smutty ones?

Fuck, I need to get laid. This is stupid.

I ignore her text for a couple of hours until another message from her pops up.

EVE:

Hello? Are you ignoring me?

I'd better reply so she'll stop texting me. Goddamn, she'd be a handful. Grunting, I stab at the screen, then tap at the tiny fucking letters.

DEREK:

Sorry, just saw this. I'll be there. Should I bring anything?

EVE:

Just yourself. Cole said to come at seven.

My fingers hover over the screen as I debate how to reply. I'm curious about what she's doing today. Sighing, I type out what I know I should say.

DEREK:

K. See you then.

I stare at my phone, wondering if she'll reply. When it doesn't vibrate, I'm annoyed. What the hell is wrong with me? I'm acting like some twitterpated teen.

I've never been one to think that dominant men have to control every moment of the day, but my body's reaction to her isn't normal. How did she throw me off balance this fast? I thought she was smoking hot at the party, and then one car trip with her later, I'm as twitchy as a heroin addict.

If she hadn't started questioning me about BDSM practices and saying she wanted to fuck without a commitment, I wouldn't be considering giving her what she wants. If she was anyone but Cole's sister, I wouldn't hesitate. I'm not going to marry someone a decade younger than me—or at all, to be honest. But I'd be up for a little fun with a sexy woman a few years out of college.

I grab my phone again and continue to scroll through the names of my contacts. I have a couple of women who are friends with benefits when we're both single. A little physical activity will take the edge off my thoughts about Evie, and then I can be a regular platonic friend on Saturday night.

I scroll past each name, but nothing feels right. After mentally crossing off every woman on the list, I'm disgusted with myself. I've already given into the fantasy and masturbated thinking of her. If I do that again, I'll never get her out of my head.

Okay, new plan. Make it through Saturday, and I'll never see her again. I've lived in town for years and never run into her before. I spend the rest of the night trying to ignore the itch in the back of my mind that tells me Evie seems different from anyone I've met.

CHAPTER 9
Derek

The sun is still out as I pull into Cole's parents' driveway. It's a beautiful evening with a gentle breeze—perfect weather for relaxing with friends. He texted me earlier and said that the door was unlocked and that he'd be on the back deck working at the grill.

I knock to warn anyone near the door, then open it and call out. "Hey, Cole?"

Evie peeks out from an archway that leads to the kitchen. "Oh, hi!"

She looks fucking fantastic, wearing a low-cut blue sundress that shows off her perky breasts and dances around her firm thighs. This will be a long evening, especially with her in that dress. But it doesn't have to be awkward if we both play along with the charade that we're old family friends and there's nothing sexual going on between us.

"Hi, Eve."

She smiles seductively, making me wonder if she's still trying to get me to fuck her. In that dress, it won't take much to distract me from my sudden obsession with celibacy. I cough and then return to an all-business attitude.

"Is Cole in the back?"

"Nah." She wrinkles her nose, and her eyes sparkle like she knows a secret. "Cole's running late. So it's just you and me."

Just us? This isn't good. She bites her lip, and it's so damn sexy, it makes me want to bite it for her.

Fuck, get a grip, Derek.

We're just two people hanging out for dinner until her brother shows up. I can do this. It's only an hour or two, tops. I pride myself on not losing control. Pushing away my carnal thoughts, I know I can withstand Evie's teasing for that long. Even if I already want to tear that dress off her shoulders and trail kisses down her naked body, telling her all the filthy things I'd do to her....

Jesus, fuck, c'mon brain, help me out a little.

I close my eyes and inhale slowly. When I open them and step past her, she brushes against me, and I freeze. She doesn't back away, and I resist my body's impulsive reaction. After a pause, I keep walking toward the sliding door that leads outside. "I'll be waiting out here."

Once outside I try calming my nerves and convince myself this will be okay. I almost reach the grill before Eve joins me. Shoving my hands in my pockets, I face her as she rests against a wooden chair, her hands resting beside her hips. It's obvious she isn't wearing a bra. The fabric clings to her nipples, and I can see their stiff points through the material. I don't know what game she thinks she's playing, but she's obviously flirting with me. She's making my cock hard as hell with the dress, the lip biting, the fucking citrus vanilla perfume. Dammit, am I gonna have to talk to her about how nothing is going to happen between us again?

Her phone rings, and she picks it up from the table beside her and answers it. "Yo, where are you? Derek's here."

There's a pause, and then Eve laughs. "You're such a jerk."

After a few moments of back and forth, she hangs up and smiles at me. "So, Cole just bailed on us. He said something came up, and he'd explain it later."

She pushes off the chair and saunters closer to me, her hips rolling, and I feel like I'm her prey and she's the dominant one. This is bad—really, really bad. Her tone is sultry yet playful, as she speaks slowly. "Looks like it's going to be just you and me...all night."

This isn't an innocent invitation to spend time playing fucking Uno. She has no intention of stopping her flirtations, just testing my resolve. I take a deep breath and try to stay calm and composed. I have to end this right now before it gets out of hand. "Eve, we talked about this."

Eve doesn't stop smiling, and her eyes sparkle mischievously. "What? We're just two people who're gonna enjoy a meal. It's not wrong to have dinner together."

She's a handful, and her boldness is driving me insane. To be honest, I enjoy the challenge of a bratty sub—pushing them to the point of begging for what they want. But this is all backward. Upside down. Fucking sideways, and it's getting ridiculous. "Listen, Eve—" I lose my train of thought as Eve peers up at me innocently, slowly blinking like a fucking kitten.

"Yes?"

Jesus. This is harder than I thought it would be. I want her too much, and it's screwing with me. But she can't act like this around dominant guys. Even worse would be the insufferable, confident younger dudes who know nothing about BDSM. The idiots who just want kinky sex, like her. My brain lights up as I work through the calculus. She could get hurt if I don't help her understand.

I take a step back to distance myself from her. "If you want to be in the lifestyle, you gotta learn some things. You can't behave like this. This could be misinterpreted by some assholes."

Eve tilts her head at me. "Pft, lifestyle. It's just a kinky game, right?—roleplaying? Besides, we're alone."

A game, huh? She's toying with me, and it's working. The way she plays with one of the spaghetti straps of her sundress and that sexy smirk. Fuck. My mind spins as I think of pulling down the bodice of her dress, baring those breasts, and feasting on them. My resolve snaps. I want her, and there's only so much I can take. This bratty submissive should be taught a lesson.

"Fine." I stalk over and crowd her, staring down at her, daring her to break our connection first. I smile when her expression sharpens—she's not blinking now. "You think this is just a game? Let's play a little more, okay, Evie? If you can look me in the eye and tell me you're a slut and want to be used like one, I'll fuck you."

Eve swallows, breathing in shallow pants. She licks her lips, then smiles slowly. "I'm a slut."

I grunt derisively since she didn't fully respond. It's even more clear to me she doesn't know what she's in for. I should turn and walk away, but I can't. I want to see how she responds when she realizes this isn't a game to me. "And?"

Eve raises an eyebrow, pretending to be confused while coyly watching me. "And what?"

When I grab her ass and haul her into my body, her eyes widen in surprise as she moans. Her hands press lightly against my chest, and I inhale her scent. Steadying my gaze, I lower to a deeper register. "Say it. Use your words, baby girl. Tell me what you want."

Eve's face flushes and she watches me hungrily. "Fuck me, please?"

I relax my grip on her round, firm bottom, wrapping my arms around the small of her back, leaning into her, kissing her neck softly, trailing towards her ear. When I whisper, "That wasn't what I said, Evie. Repeat the entire phrase so I know what you want. Are you a slut who wants to be used like one?" Her body jerks with pleasure, and she lets out a gasp. "Well?" I growl.

Eve's hoarse when she answers, "Yes, I want to be used like a slut."

"Sir."

She gasps at my gruff demand before mumbling, "Sir."

That's all I need to hear. But I'm not ready to drop it after her bratty responses.

"The whole thing again. Don't fuck with me. Look me in the eye, and say it like you mean it."

She freezes before her gaze slowly rises and we lock onto each other. Softly yet steady she tells me what she wants. "I'm a slut, and I want to be used like one—by you. Sir."

I can't turn away from her. She stares at me without the teasing glint from earlier and holds her breath. When I pull her tighter against me, and grind my stiffness along her core, she whimpers, pushes her hips forward, dragging her hot mound over my rigid shaft. I resist the impulse to twist her around, bend her over the picnic table behind her, and rail her right where we stand.

Letting go of her, I step back a few paces. I've gotta keep my resolve and stick to the plan forming in my mind. It's not going to be just sex, and she deserves my best.

As I close the distance, she steps back, but her ass hits the edge of the table and she stops. Grabbing her hips, I pick her up and set her on the surface. I spread her knees apart with my hands and trail a finger along her inner thigh from her knee towards her core.

"Do you remember what I told you in the car?"

Eve's irises haze with lust as we stare at each other. Her neck moves in slow motion, bobbing as she speaks, "Mm hmm, yes."

"What was it?" I slide the material of her panties aside and run my fingertip along the hem, teasing her pussy lips. Her eyelids drift closed, and she moans at my touch. I pull my hand away, and she whimpers, her hips arching toward me.

"Say it, or I stop."

Eve's eyes snap open, and she stares at me with a mixture of passion and annoyance. "Derek!"

I smirk and raise an eyebrow, waiting.

"You said you worship your subs and take care of them."

My brain buzzes at her words. She remembered exactly what I'd said. I thought she was playing games, but she paid attention to me at every turn, and that's something new. Her confidence is remarkable, and I'm going to make sure she feels worshipped.

"Good girl. Now, listen to me."

She tries to concentrate on me but her eyes drift down my body to where I'm standing between her spread thighs. I know she'll love anything I do to her. I take my time lowering to kiss her while finding her clit and rubbing my fingertip in lazy circles. I whisper against her lips. "You're not my sub, Evie. But I'll give you a taste of what it would be like."

She groans, "Please."

Eve wraps her legs around mine, digging her heels into my ass, trying to pull me closer, but I stay where I am—kissing her, enjoying her. I take my time circling her tender nub with my finger. When my light touch changes, pressing firmly against her bundle of nerves, she sucks in a ragged breath, her thighs trembling.

When her head drops back she tightens her legs, raising her ass off the table. I know she's close to coming, so I slow down my movement. "You said you wanted me to use you like a slut—"

Eve frowns at me in confusion as our eyes meet after I trail off. She shimmies her hips, grinding on my hand. "Yes, please. Use me."

I pull my hand away from her heated sex, and she mewls in distress. When I take another step away from her, a tiny line appears between her eyebrows that I want to kiss and soothe.

Shifting to the side behind a deck chair, I face her. "I will use you like a slut, Evie. But I want you to understand something first."

"What's that?" She sits up straighter but keeps her legs spread.

With my gaze locked on hers, I notice her hiked up dress with her panties pulled to the side revealing her glistening pussy. Her nipples strain against the light cotton of her sundress and her face is flush with arousal. I fight the impulse to concentrate solely on her nubile body. I must be resolute and steady as I explain how this works. I'm in my element, and a sense of power rushes through my nerves. This is why I enjoy the BDSM scene—how power shifts between us as we dance. I study her, and she squirms under my gaze.

"You are a slut," I finally say. "It's as simple as that. This isn't something I make you feel—it's already inside you. You can't turn it off and on, but you can control it. I will give you a safe place to release your inner slut. Is that what you want?"

She nods slowly as understanding flares in her darkening expression. I move the chair in front of her, sit down, and tuck my hands underneath her thighs, pulling her closer to the edge. Her intoxicating citrus and vanilla perfume mixing with the scent of her leaking desire makes me want to devour her.

"One last thing." I kiss the inside of her thigh softly as my thumb circles the same spot on her other thigh. "You're a slut. But I'm in charge. I'll decide how to make you fall apart—not you. You're going to get hooked on it, Evie. I'm gonna start by licking your pretty little pussy." Her eyes widen, and before she can respond, I tell her, "Relax, baby girl, and enjoy the ride."

CHAPTER 10

Eve

Oh my god—Derek's going to lick me?

A rush of electricity jolts through me, tightening every muscle, making it impossible to relax. No one's ever gone down on me before, and I have no idea what I'm supposed to do. Say something? Stay still?

He hooks his fingers under the waistband of my panties and slowly eases them down my legs, his touch maddeningly gentle. Then his mouth trails kisses up the inside of my thigh, each one setting off sparks under my skin.

When he finally pauses, his eyes flick up to meet mine. There's a secretive little grin tugging at his lips, like he knows exactly how wrecked I already am. "Ready, baby girl?"

I'm vibrating with lust. Leaning back, I rest my elbows on the table but keep watching the sexy man. Oh god, what if I don't like this, or what if I taste bad?

A throb of desire pulses through me, and as he presses a tender kiss to the top of my mound, it tickles, and I relax. He's probably done this tons of times. I'll just trust that he knows he enjoys it.

When he spreads open my labia with his thumbs and swirls his tongue around my clit, I suck in my breath as pleasure courses through me.

"Ohhhh, god," I gasp, my toes curling as delight ripples up my spine.

Derek pulls away, his expression unreadable.

Shit, did I do something wrong? "Sorry," I mumble.

"Baby, I'm only watching your pleasure. You're fine."

He dips down again and licks along my slit, sending shockwaves of bliss through me.

Derek purrs, "There you go, baby girl. Just enjoy it. Let yourself go, release the inner slut."

As his tongue explores my folds and slips inside, I reach for his head with one hand, trying to get him to press harder against me. "Oh god, please."

Derek grabs my wrist and forces my arm to my sides. "Just lie back while I devour you."

Fuck, how does he expect me not to touch him? He's driving me insane.

I ease back onto the table, the wood cool against my spine, the night air brushing over my overheated skin. I clutch the edges, trying to anchor myself as he explores every inch of me with his tongue. The sensation is too much—sharp, tender, and addictive. An unfamiliar urge coils tighter inside me with every flick and swirl.

When his fingers press into my pussy and his lips tighten around my clit, I let out a broken, desperate sound—nonsense words tumbling from my mouth as bliss crashes through me like a wave.

Derek laughs, the vibration a warm puff against my skin. "You taste so fucking good, Evie."

I'm about ready to beg him for more, but his tongue between my legs is turning my brain to mush and it's impossible to find the words. "Derek..."

He pauses. "What's the magic word?"

Uh… did he tell me a word? My brain's too foggy to think. "Sir? Please? More? God, don't stop!"

He lifts my legs over his shoulders and nuzzles deeper into my folds. His tongue flutters and circles my clit, each pass making my body jolt.

"Good girl," he murmurs. "You picked the right word."

Before I can even wonder which word worked, he sucks firmly on my clit, grazing it lightly with his teeth. I cry out, hips bucking against his mouth, wordlessly begging for more.

I can't hold back, and I cry out as an orgasm hits me so hard that my whole body trembles. Pleasure ripples from my fingers to my toes and I flex my hips, grinding my pussy into his face, desperate to experience each second of bliss. My heart races as a euphoric high continues to rush through me. Oh god, I've never come this hard.

My body stops shaking, and when Derek kisses the insides of my thighs, I tremble with tiny aftershocks of pleasure. I've never felt this alive, and it's not just the orgasms, but being with him and knowing he wants me.

Derek speaks, and his words are thick with emotion. "You taste delicious. I'm not sure I want to stop."

I'm still trying to process what just happened, but I won't stop him if he keeps going.

Derek's tongue traces patterns along the outside of my pussy, teasing and tormenting me.

I whimper, "Please?"

"What was that?" The question comes out muffled as he kisses my pussy.

When he slides his fingers inside me, my entire body jerks in pleasure, and I gasp, "Derek!"

He pauses long enough to look at me with insatiable lust. "Do you want me?"

"Yes, please," I moan out, rotating my hips to tempt him. Will he fuck me right here on the table?

It's as if he can read my mind when he growls against my skin, "You have no idea of all the things I want to do to you."

Derek's hands slide under my dress, pushing the fabric higher. The material brushes against my skin, sending tiny shivers across my body as he reveals more of me. He trails hot, lingering kisses along my hips, working his way up, each touch is a slow torment that makes me gasp.

When he finally pushes the dress up to my shoulders, baring my breasts to the cool night air, he pauses to admire me. I flush from embarrassment, but I force myself to keep my hands at my sides, resisting the instinct to cover myself.

Then his mouth closes over one of my nipples, sucking gently before giving a playful bite. A sharp jolt of pleasure shoots through me, and I cry out, arching up into him, desperate for more.

His eyes crinkle with impish delight. "So sensitive. So beautiful. Such a needy slut."

I try to stay still as his tongue swirls around my nipple. When he's done with one, he kisses through the valley between my breasts to reach the other. The second nipple is extra sensitive, primed and ready for his mouth, and when he sucks hard, a wave of pleasurable pain rushes through me.

"Fuuuuck. More!"

He chuckles. "That's up to me, baby girl. I might just tease you all night long. Just nibble and savor the taste of you. It doesn't matter what I do. You're going to lie here and take whatever I give you."

I'm dizzy at his words because I know he's right. I'm spellbound with pleasure, and I'll just lie here for as long as he continues to worship me. He leans over me, supporting himself on one arm, and when he kisses my neck, goosebumps rise along my skin. His touch is like a caress.

"So sweet, and all mine." I feel his words vibrate against my skin.

Mmm. For this much pleasure, I really will do anything he wants. He kisses me gently, and it's intoxicating. I melt under him, feeling completely at ease and safe. Tentatively, I run my tongue along his lips and he deepens the kiss. When his fingers find my clit again, I break the kiss to moan.

"There we go. Just give into it, slut. I've got you."

He dips two fingers inside me, exploring every inch of my pussy. I close my eyes, allowing myself to succumb to the intense delight. When he curls his fingers and massages a magical spot, I convulse and cry out in pleasure.

"Ohhh, god!"

"Mmm, you like that? You like my fingers fucking your slutty pussy?"

Spikes of delight ping up and down my body, and I'm desperate for him to give me more. "Please?"

As he cycles his thick digits in and out of me, Derek kisses and sucks on my neck. He finds the sensitive skin just below my earlobe and I shudder as I edge closer to another orgasm.

When he rubs the most perfect spot inside me, the dam breaks, and I come undone. I scream out as waves of pleasure roll over me and my pussy contracts, trying to hold on to his fingers.

"Good girl," he says, and continues to finger fuck me through my orgasm. "Yes, let go, give it to me. Give me all of it. It's mine now."

After the tremors stop, I'm sprawled on the table, exhausted. Derek grins like he's proud of himself—no, like he's proud of me and delighted that I let out my inner slut.

I'm not sure what to say. Is he done? Does he want me to suck on him? Should I offer to take him into the house? Before I can speak, he stands up and pulls me up with him, wrapping his arms around me. He hugs me tenderly. "That was beautiful."

This is the first time a guy has hugged me after something sexual. Todd would just immediately get up and leave me after I gave him a blowjob. When Derek plants a kiss on my head, my heart races. What's happening to me?

Derek's reply holds an edge of authority that makes me quiver. "Baby girl, do you have any idea how desperately I want to fuck you right now?"

Then why isn't he?

He affectionately strokes his thumb over my cheek. "I'm not going to do that, Evie. Not yet."

I blink and stare at him, unsure if I heard him right. Why the hell not? I just gave him the green light, and he made me come, like, a bunch of times. Now I want to give him pleasure.

"But I want more..." I whisper, feeling close to tears.

Derek strokes my cheek again, then pulls me in for another hug. When I lean into his embrace, he whispers into my ear, "Baby girl, I'm not done with you, but you deserve to be worshipped."

He keeps using that word, and it makes me tremble with desire while I whisper, "I feel that way. Now, I want to make you happy."

Derek pauses as if mentally debating something. After a few moments, I can feel his body relax, as if he's giving in.

"Then let's go to your bedroom so I can do this right."

CHAPTER 11

Eve

As I lead him to my room, I can't stop thinking about what he meant by "doing it right." The way he licked me? That already felt perfect. What more could he possibly do to top that?

Inside, he pauses, eyes flicking around my bedroom—and then he grins.

Oh fuck. Is it too childish? My posters, my stuffed animals, the pink sheets I never bothered to replace when I came home from college. I suddenly feel ashamed of not changing my room to reflect my adult status. He doesn't need any more reminders of how much younger I am.

But then he shuts the door. Oooh, guess it's okay after all. It's game on.

He regards me with a steady, penetrating gaze. "Take off your dress."

Like...right now? Just strip? My hesitation must show, because his tone softens into something coaxing. "Be a good girl and take your clothes off so I can admire that gorgeous body of yours."

I giggle, giddy and buzzing as I remove my dress. It slides to the floor, and I'm suddenly so aware of my nakedness. I cross one arm over my chest, the other over my stomach, feeling vulnerable and not nearly pretty enough. All those model-perfect women at the party–I'm not like them. Not polished. Not flawless.

Derek steps in close, and I stumble back until my calves hit the bed. He takes my wrists and pulls my arms away from my body, baring me completely.

"You're so fucking gorgeous," he says. "Never hide yourself from me. Celebrate it."

Something breaks open in me, and a warm ripple skates down my spine. Then he nudges me down onto the mattress, and I prop myself up on my elbows, watching.

He strips. Slowly. His entire body is unreal—tight abs, muscles like a sculpture. I knew he was hot, but this? He's a fucking god.

He catches me staring and smirks. "You like?"

"Mm hmm," I breathe.

Derek grabs my knees and drags me to the edge of the bed. My legs fall open around him. "Baby girl, you look fucking delicious."

I whimper, desperate. His cock rubs against my slick folds, teasing, gliding, but not pressing in. Why is he waiting? Oh.

"Please, Derek," I beg.

That's all it takes.

He thrusts into me, and I gasp—holy shit, he's huge. My body clenches around him, stretched and full, lit up from the inside. I expected pain with my first time, but this is only plea-sure. And I want more.

When he pulls out completely. I whine, thrashing my head. "Oh god, please!"

He grins down at me, and rubs his cock over my entrance again. "Please what?"

"Fuck me! Please, fuck me!"

And he does. Deep, steady strokes that rock my entire body and make my breasts bounce. He pulls my legs up and rests my ankles on his shoulders as he drives into me. I'm soaking wet, and I moan in an increasing crescendo with every smack of his hips.

"So beautiful, taking my cock like a good girl."

His words make me blush and clench around him. I want to be good. I want to make him lose control. "Fuck me harder."

He growls and pounds into me. His grasp on my thighs tightens. "You're such a slut for my cock, baby girl."

"Yes," I gasp. "Your slut. Oh fuck, harder, please!"

He snarls and slams into me like he wants to break the bed. I clutch the blanket, trying not to fly off the mattress. It's brutal and perfect and I want more.

When he shifts his weight and changes the angle, he hits something deep that makes my eyes roll back. "Ohhh god!"

"Eyes on me, baby girl."

I force my eyes open, and my whole body trembles. It's too much. Too intense. Too intimate. And I love it.

His thrusts slow. "Rub your clit, needy girl. Come on my cock like a good slut."

Oh god. I reach down, rubbing tight circles over my clit. His cock keeps dragging over every nerve ending inside me, and the eye contact holds me captive. I feel beautiful. Desired. Owned.

"That's it," he whispers. "That's my good girl."

My legs shake. My breath catches. I'm so close.

Then he pushes my knees towards my shoulders and drives in deeper, hitting that perfect spot again and again. I can't stop crying out. I'm poised at the precipice ready to explode as my hand moves faster.

"Please!" I beg. "Please let me come!"

"Come for me, baby," he says, and that's all it takes.

I shatter. My pussy clenches around him as my orgasm rips through me, loud and blinding. I tremble and gasp while he continues to fuck me. His face tightens as he groans and thrusts deeper, chasing his own high.

With a shout, Derek slams in one last time and holds there,

pulsing inside me. I can feel his cock emptying, thick spurts of cum coating my insides. It goes on forever. I moan at the thought of being so full of him.

When he finally finishes, he pulls out slowly and collapses beside me, dragging me into his arms. I'm floating in the warmth of his body and the afterglow.

Everything's perfect.

Fucking my brother's friend was the best decision I ever made.

CHAPTER 12
Derek

W hat just happened? My thoughts drift unformed as I hold Evie against my chest. Spooning after sex or a hard play session is normal. It's an excellent way to make the sub feel safe during aftercare. But I can't pull Evie close enough. I want to drag her body inside me. I want to get drunk with her presence. I center on slowing my breathing as I begin to understand the trouble I'm in. It was too good, the best sex I've had in ages—in my life.

So I quiet my head and try to ignore how our bodies tangle together, lax in warm, contented bliss. I could lie here forever, brushing my fingers through Evie's hair, caressing her warm humid skin, and relishing the calm that washes over me. Being with her like this is so tranquil. It's been a while since a woman has made me feel peaceful after sex. After a few moments, Evie's breathing grows deep and even, and I'm positive she's asleep. That's fine—it's still early. I'm not surprised she's passed out after such an intense fuck.

As my body sinks further into relaxation, I almost drift off. A nagging thought tugs at the base of my skull—I don't want to go back home. I never think like this. Even while I was with Jenny, we rarely shared a bed after sex. This isn't how things usually work for me. When I'm done with a scene with a sub, we cuddle for a bit for aftercare, say a few pleasantries before we go our separate ways. It's been forever since I've had a woman fall asleep in my arms. But this? It feels natural and right to have Eve snuggled against me.

When I kiss the top of her head, she hums a soft purr. I smile, enjoying the sensation of her body spooned inside mine. My worries evaporate when I realize this is where she belongs—she's mine. I should have known it was inevitable when I gave her a ride from my shop. When she told me what she wanted, I felt a visceral response. There's no point in fighting it anymore. I want her, and I will have her.

What happens after tonight? That thought pings again. More —that's what I want. More of Evie. More of us. What else could I possibly think? I want… something I've never wanted before.

After a short time, I untangle myself, and though I try not to wake her as I slip out of bed, Evie whimpers, and I feel guilty for disturbing her. As I tuck the blankets around her shoulders, I whisper, "Go back to sleep." She nods but doesn't open her eyes. Her breathing returns to normal within moments, and her body stays still. As I stare at her serene face as I stand over her, I have a sense of pride that she feels safe enough to rest peacefully. She's not agitated or worried. This is how it should be between us.

I visit the bathroom to clean up and return to her bedside to put my clothes on. Cole could come back, and I shouldn't be walking around her house buck-ass naked.

The countless nights with different girls replay in my thoughts. They'd enjoy a cuddle, then want distance, pushing me inexorably away. I was the same. I kept them at arm's length, open to another tangle, but to spend the night? Never. We'd had sex, and that's all it ever was. It was physical and enjoyable, but it didn't go past that. With Evie, the impulse to leave is absent.

After snatching my phone from the pocket in my jeans crumpled on Evie's floor, I step outside the bedroom, closing the door quietly behind me. I'm going to stay the night, and Eve and I will talk in the morning. It's impossible to walk away from her right now. Not with the way my heart tightens at the thought of her waking and finding me gone.

It happened so quickly. We didn't discuss anything beforehand, and we didn't use a condom. Fuck, is she on birth control? We'll have to talk about that too, Jesus. I'm always careful with protection and only go bareback with subs after we've both been tested. Getting one of them pregnant was my biggest fear. It would change my life drastically. But everything is different with Evie, and I'm going to keep seeing her and fuck, so what if we had a little tyke?

What the fuck is going on?

What in the hell am I going to tell Cole?

Pacing around the living room, I contemplate texting him and just admitting what happened, but there's no good way to say, "Hey man, I fucked your sister, and now she's passed out from bliss. Oh, and by the way, you could be an uncle in nine months."

Jesus, why doesn't that freak me out?

She's mine. I'm not going to let her go. I'll take care of her, make her happy. If this reckless night pulls us together with an unplanned pregnancy, we'll deal with it. Hell, I'll even…

What the fuck?

I tell myself to calm down; it's not even midnight yet. I'll figure everything out tomorrow. I'll stay with her tonight so she can see me beside her when she wakes up. Then we'll discuss things, we'll tell Cole about our being together, and then proceed from there. Satisfied with my decision, I head to the kitchen so I can make something to eat. A sandwich is the quickest thing, and there's not much else to choose from in the fridge.

Tonight didn't turn out how I expected. I figured dinner and some joking around with Evie and Cole. Maybe watch a movie or play cards, just the three of us. Instead, Cole is off doing whatever the fuck he's doing, and Evie and I end up in her bed having life-altering sex.

Okay, sure. Evie isn't as experienced in BDSM as I initially thought, but I'm eager to teach her everything she wants. Fuck, I'll make her a perfect sub. I chuckle, knowing she'll still be a brat, but she'll be *my* brat. I'll show her patience even as she teases and taunts me, knowing she'll seek the safety of my presence. All I want is for her to be mine, and I can't even think of anyone else. My cock stirs just thinking about her being my willing submissive. I'm drunk on the idea of it and have to push away the stray thought that tells me she's more than just my sub.

Once I eat, I guzzle a bottle of water, then bring two more bottles with me upstairs. Evie is still asleep as I carefully lock the door behind me silently. I place the bottles on the nightstand before removing my clothes. When I slide into bed beside her, she immediately rolls into me, nuzzling into my chest and sleepily kissing along my neck before brushing her lips to mine.

I rest my hands on her waist as my cock stiffens, the shaft lengthening between us and pressing against her thigh. The beast in me wants to roll her over and fuck her until she's senseless, but her even breathing tells me she's gone back to sleep. An aching cock all night will be worth it if I wake up beside her. I try to empty my head, concentrating on blackness, but it's a long time before I can fall asleep.

When I wake up, Evie lies against me, watching her finger as she twirls my chest hair. I capture her hand and press it against my chest, causing her to giggle.

Her eyes lift and her cheeks are flush with happiness when she whispers, "Good morning."

74

"Hey, you." I grin.

We gaze at each other for a few moments, and I enjoy how adorable she is with her bed head and sleepy expression. There's so much I want to ask her, and we're going to talk seriously about our relationship, but not yet—not this minute. Not while the morning sun shines through her bedroom window, making everything seem peaceful and perfect.

Instead, I kiss her softly. We both laugh when her stomach rumbles. "Let's get you fed." I roll off the bed and stand up, stretching out my muscles. "I'll cook you breakfast."

Evie sits up. "Oh! Do you have time?"

I grin at her. "I've got time. I'm all yours today, baby girl."

A smile lights up her face, and she hops to her feet, hurrying to the bathroom across the hall as she calls over her shoulder. "I'm going to take a quick shower."

This girl will be a handful, and thinking of her invading my life excites me. It doesn't hurt that she's gorgeous and has a rocking body. I anticipate exploring her curves and finding every sweet spot that will make her moan with pleasure. My body responds, but I recognize I should do something besides fantasizing about Evie naked in her shower.

After getting dressed, I head downstairs to find ingredients for pancakes. Okay, well, I spotted a large bag of pancake mix when I made my sandwich. Luckily, it's the add water kind because they're out of milk. But I find butter and half a bottle of maple-flavored syrup. As I'm mixing the batter, I wonder what she's been eating while her parents are away. Maybe I'll go shopping for her; her fridge is fucking empty.

I shake my head and grumble to myself. What the fuck was that?

I'm flipping pancakes when I hear her on the stairs and glance over my shoulder as Evie turns at the bottom of the stairs. She's wearing cutoffs and a loose T-shirt that says, "Kiss me, I'm Irish." Smiling brightly, she walks over and wraps her arms around me, rises on her toes to kiss behind my ear. I close my eyes when I feel her breasts flatten against my back. Quiet intimacy is something I've missed by never sleeping over, and I want more of this with Evie.

After I flip the last pancake, I turn to hug her. "Are you always this perky in the morning?"

Evie smiles up at me, her eyes sparkling, and shakes her head. "Nah, I just woke up in a good mood. I don't know why." She shrugs like she wasn't moaning in passion while we fucked last night.

Jesus, this girl is too adorable. I lean and kiss her, tracing my tongue along her bottom lip, teasing her until she opens her mouth and invites me in. I press her against the counter, and we're lost in a passionate kiss, exploring each other's mouths. I grab her ass, and she lifts her foot behind my knee, practically crawling up my body. I'm about to hoist her onto the edge and spread her open when the smell of something burning pulls me away and back to reality.

I reach and shut off the burner, then turn back to her. "I burnt your pancake."

Eve is panting, and her nipples are visibly hard through her T-shirt. "Who cares?"

She slides her hands around my neck and drags me back down to her mouth. I'm a goner. I can't resist her. I grab her hips, lifting her onto the counter, and she hooks her ankles behind my thighs. Fuck, she's so sexy, and I want to bury myself inside her.

When the front door slams open, I jump back from her. Shit!

Cole strides into the kitchen, whistling. He halts when he sees me standing an arm's length away from Evie, sitting on the counter with her legs open. He peers at the burnt pancakes, and a stormy expression passes over his face. He glares at Evie first and then at me.

"So, do you guys have something to tell me?"

CHAPTER 13

Eve

I stare at Cole while my brain scrambles for words. I could say, "Oh god, it's not what it looks like!" or maybe, "Yes, your best friend took my virginity last night and rearranged my fucking soul." Something. Anything. But nothing comes out.

Derek steps between us. He's calm and controlled. "Eve and I are seeing each other."

I shiver and wish that were true—or at least planning to fuck some more.

Cole sputters. "You're seeing her? Since when?"

Derek just shrugs, casual as hell, and I suddenly feel guilty. This is my mess, and he shouldn't have to take the fall.

"One of Jasper's parties," I say quickly.

Cole swings his eyes to me. "When the hell were you at one of Jasper's parties?"

Oops. "I have a life, you know. I didn't think I had to check in before doing kinky shit."

He stares at me a second longer, then lets out a tired sigh. "Don't tell Mom and Dad anything. They don't know what I do, and they'd lose it."

I nod, pretending I understand what the hell he's talking about. We're not a share-your-sex-life kind of family, and I'm fine keeping it that way.

Cole turns back to Derek. "Really, man? My little sister?"

Derek spreads his hands out to his sides. "The heart wants what the heart wants."

Wait. What? I nearly fall off the damn counter. We had one incredible night. Now he's talking like this is some kind of love story.

Cole sighs, clearly frustrated. "Okay. But if you hurt her, we're done. Got it?"

"I'll never hurt her."

Derek's words thrill me. Holy shit. This is real. Cole's friendship is on the line, and Derek's not backing down.

Cole mutters something under his breath and looks at me again. "I just stopped in for a second. I have to go fix something. But seriously, don't say a word to Mom and Dad until you're, like, walking down the aisle or something. Don't make them hate Derek."

I suck in air and almost choke. Walking down the aisle?

Derek jumps in again. "We'll be careful. Promise."

They do the classic bro-hug-and-backslap, and then Cole gives Derek a long look before heading for the door.

"Don't burn the place down before Mom and Dad get back."

"Bye!" I say with the sweetest, most innocent tone I can muster.

The door slams shut, and I grin at Derek. "So…that went well, right?"

"Yeah. Not bad."

We fall into a weird silence after that. He goes back to the stove, flipping pancakes like it's just a normal morning, and I hop off the counter to set the table. While we eat, we keep stealing glances at each other and my brain won't shut off.

When I'm done, I push my chair back and stand. "Want anything?"

"I'm good."

Cool cool cool. So…are we going to fuck again or what? I'm not brave enough to ask.

I clean up while he finishes eating, trying not to overanalyze, but it's impossible. I want to ask where this is going, but I'm terrified of the answer.

When he finally steps up behind me and wraps his arms around my waist, I melt instantly. He buries his face in my neck. "What's wrong, baby girl? I can hear you thinking."

I laugh, and the tension eases a little. "What do we do now?"

His breath is hot against my skin. "Anything we want."

God, that sounds good. "What if I wanted you to be my dom? To train me?"

He spins me around, and the look he gives me makes my legs weak. "Ask me."

My heart pounds. "Will you train me as your submissive and make me yours?"

"You're already mine."

Heat blooms everywhere as he hugs me tight, then takes my hand and leads me upstairs. He closes the door behind us, and I almost joke and ask him who he's expecting to walk in.

"Strip." His eyes are unreadable, and I shiver.

Oh fuck. This is happening.

I'm naked in seconds and my body hums while my heart pounds. He watches from the middle of the room with undisguised hunger.

Then he sits on the bed and crooks a finger. "Come here, baby girl."

I go to him instantly, and he pulls me into his lap, kissing me slow and deep.

"I love that you're mine."

The way he says it makes my whole body ache.

He looks up at me. "Do you know what that means? To belong to me?"

My, "No," comes out breathless.

His eyes flash. "I could bend you over and fuck you right now until you forget your own name."

Um… yes… "Please," I moan. He tweaks my nipple and I gasp, hips twitching.

"I want to teach you so many things…."

My thighs are trembling and my pussy's already clenching on nothing. It's crazy how quickly he can turn me into a desperate little slut.

He nudges me to my feet and guides me across the room to the old desk tucked under the window, the same one I used to do homework at, still cluttered with leftover pieces of my childhood. A cracked snow globe, a chipped jewelry box, a few faded photos in cheap plastic frames. The familiar clutter blurs at the edges of my vision as adrenaline pulses through me.

"Turn. Bend over," Derek murmurs.

My heart hammers against my ribs as I obey and bend over the desk.

He places his hands firmly over mine, guiding them to the back edge. "Lean on your elbows," he says. "Hold on. Don't move."

"Yes, sir."

The cool surface of the desk presses into my skin as I brace myself for whatever's about to happen next. I hope he's going to fuck me like this.

Behind me, he asks, "You know what's about to happen?"

Smack!

"Oww!" I yelp as the spank rings out, a sharp sting blooming across my ass.

It hurts. But it also doesn't. It's heat and pressure and a flood of something I can't name.

He rubs the sore spot, and I look back, panting.

He grins. "Did you like that?"

I peep out a tiny, "Yes."

"Good."

Smack!

Another slap. Another wave of heat. I moan, fingers tightening on the desk as I wait for him to spank me again. I liked what he was doing and could handle more. But after a moment when nothing happens, I glance over my shoulder and wiggle my ass at him, teasing.

The look he gives me is pure darkness. What the hell is he going to do to me?

CHAPTER 14
Derek

Our eyes meet, and I'm at a crossroads about whether to continue after the first smack. The sexual chemistry we experienced last night and this morning is overwhelming. She thinks she wants to be kinky but has no experience with playing other than watching. She has no idea how she tempts me with her eyes as she sways her delicious ass like a red cape flapping in the hands of a toreador.

And I'm the fucking bull.

Determined to push her, I pull my hand back and swat her ass again, then smack the other cheek before she has time to complain. Evie cries out from the sudden impacts but lowers her head to the desk surface, as if she's surrendering. But she doesn't complain as her body relaxes, processing the pain.

I tighten my jaw. I'm not a sadist. Well, not entirely, but at this moment, I want her tears. I don't want to injure her. I'm not punishing her for anything, I crave the emotions. What a spanking releases beyond the tears. But I need to keep myself in check.

"Say 'red' if it hurts too much." I rub her bottom with my

palm tenderly, soothing her nerves. I want to show her how pain and pleasure mix, but she has a say in anything we do. She's gotta know she has the power to end what's happening to keep herself safe. She nods her head.

"Say it back to me. What word means for me to stop?"

"Red," she whines as her hips roll. "But I don't want you to stop."

I swat her ass sharply, using my free arm to hold her down on the desk, pressing against the small of her back. She yips but bites back a scream of pain. She whimpers but doesn't complain with the next harsh slap either. What is she feeling right now? I can't ask her; I'm in charge of the action and must read her body language. But she's not giving any signs of distress other than the cries of pain, fading into whimpers as she forces herself to relax.

The tension in her body from my hard smacks releases, like she's building trust in letting me continue, and that seals it for me. "This is mine," I growl, swatting her ass again. "I own this juicy ass, you understand?" I punctuate my words with another sharp smack into the meaty part of her bottom.

"Augh, fuck... Yes. It's yours." Her words are a blend of pain and desire.

She swivels her hips, inviting me to continue the rough spanking. I only wanted to check her pain response, but her instinctive reaction was too delicious for me to pause now. Sliding my hand over her ass, I study her sweet pussy; it's dripping with arousal, her petals splaying open like a blooming flower—this is turning her on. The spike in my pants tells me we're both in trouble.

She's a fucking masochist.

The realization hits me as my swats shift to rapid fire. Relaxing the force, I pepper her ass with firm smacks, aiming for one spot and reddening her bottom. She remains silent, so I shift to her other side, repeating the dizzying torrent of smacks, and by the time I'm done, she's shifting from one foot to the other, whimpering from the pain.

Soothing her reddened flesh with the palm of my hand, I pause, giving her a chance to use her safeword. But her moan of pleasure tells me she's not going to tell me to stop. Her stubborn silence reminds me I'm responsible for her safety. She's not going to tap out, and it's up to me to determine when enough is enough.

Sliding my hand down the crack of her ass, I cup her pussy, gliding my fingers over her slit, collecting her slick juices. When I tease my fingertip into her opening, she moans and I can't help pushing deeper inside her tightness. She widens her stance and pushes her hips back, until my knuckles dig into her ass cheek. My cock complains. Throbbing with jealousy, wanting to sink into her honey pot.

"This is my pussy, too, isn't it, baby girl?" I lean and growl in her ear. "Your whole body is mine. Tell me."

"God, yes! I'm yours. My pussy… my ass…my tits—"

She's babbling between moans as I finger fuck her slowly. Mentioning her tits has me salivating at the thought of sucking one rock-hard nipple between my teeth as my cock slips inside her pussy. I nearly relent, strip my jeans down, and sink into her, but part of my brain pauses.

This is what she wants, and her body is fucking begging for it. But I won't give her my dick until she asks for it. Her body language indicates consent, but I want her to say it. Greedily, I want her to beg me for my cock, then reward her when she does.

"You want my cock?" I growl, pulling my fingers from her cunt and wiping them on her thigh. "Your pussy is weeping, but I want to hear you say it."

"Oh, god. Please."

"Please, what?"

"Fuck me."

I slam my fingers back into her tight passage. "Like this?"

"Mmmnn fuck. God." She shakes her head as I give it to her

with fast jabs sluicing through her lubricated slit. She practically vibrates with lust. "No…"

"No?" I stop, pulling my fingers out of her.

"Not fingers. Cock. Please! Fuck me with your cock!"

"Good girl." Stepping back, I evaluate the way she's draped over her desk, obediently gripping the edge. Her hips dance, her reddened ass swaying while the backs of her thighs tremble like she's close to coming.

"Hands behind you," I order as I tear my jeans open and shove them and my underwear to my ankles. My cock throbs, pointing right at her dripping slit. She leans forward, her head nearly over the far edge of the desk as she sweeps her hands behind her and holds her wrists at the small of her back. I step forward, gripping them tight with one hand and positioning the tip of my cock with the other. I tease her opening, but I can't resist, and I thrust firmly forward, stretching her tight entrance as I plunge into her heated depths.

"Oh, fuck! YES!" she cries as I start to rut into her.

My thighs smack the reddened cheeks of her ass, and her pussy ripples around my cock, reminding me she's already close to the edge. Still holding her wrists with one hand, I push my fingers through her hair with the other, tighten my grip and yank her head back. My hips continue to punch into her, cycling my dick as she moans out from my relentless strokes.

"You're my slut." I growl, leaning toward her ear with her upper body arched back in my grip. Her tits sway across the desk and I almost let go of her hair to grasp one of those tempting orbs. "Say it."

"Your slut. I'm your slut!"

"Do you love when I fuck you, Evie?" I growl, her responses pushing me closer as her body stiffens, and her thighs tighten. She nods wildly, but is so fucking close to coming she can't speak.

I let go of her wrists, and she's so far gone she doesn't move them from the small of her back. I wrap my arm around her thigh and strum her clit as I continue to rail her against the desk. She angles her eyes back, and we stare at each other.

"Ask me. Beg me," I say, seeing her on edge, ready to explode.

"Make me come! Please, I want to come for you!"

"Come," I growl, and her body stiffens, shaking the desk as she comes apart beautifully. Her eyes close as her mouth opens wide in a silent scream.

I ram deep inside her and release, not caring about anything but filling her up—breeding her. I can't help myself. She's mine. I'm claiming her. I'm never going to let her go. My thoughts evaporate as my hips jerk, spilling my seed into her slick channel until my balls are as empty as my mind.

I loosen my grip, and her head slowly falls against the wooden surface. I slide my hand from between her quivering thighs and stroke over her hot, red bottom and along her back. I rest my weight on top of her back as I catch my breath. Reaching between us, I pull her hands from behind her back. Entwining our fingers, I rest our arms on the desk as our breathing slows.

"Mine." My eyes blink as my thoughts return, and I realize how deeply I mean it. She's *mine*.

"Yours." She smiles as I kiss behind her ear, and her sigh is like a song as her eyes close.

CHAPTER 15

Eve

Derek's body drapes over mine, his weight grounding me in the best way. I'm floating somewhere between bliss and disbelief. I just had the most mind-blowing sex of my life. Twice. In less than twenty-four hours.

"You okay?" he whispers against my shoulder, lips brushing my skin.

I hum, "So good."

He slowly pulls out, and my body is still pulsing from pleasure. His cum leaks down my leg. My ass stings. I'm an absolute mess, and I feel amazing.

He steadies me with his hands, turning me to face him. His gaze rakes over me, equal parts heat and tenderness.

Then he directs me toward the bed. "Lie down."

I crawl into the sheets, face down, and melt into the mattress. I'm boneless and dazed.

Water runs in the bathroom. When he returns, he's holding a warm washcloth.

"Turn over for me."

I do, wincing as my sore ass brushes the sheets. He sits beside me and gently cleans between my legs. The care in the gesture guts me more than the orgasm did.

"Thank you," I whisper.

"This is part of it. Aftercare matters."

He tosses the cloth aside and lies down, pulling me onto his chest. His fingers trace light patterns on my back, calming the storm in my body. I never knew sex could feel like this. Like safety and euphoria tangled up in the same breath.

"How're you feeling?"

"Amazing," I murmur. "A little sore, but so good."

He chuckles, the sound rumbling through me. "The spanking wasn't too much?"

It wasn't enough. "I liked it. A lot."

My face heats, but he doesn't laugh.

"Some people are wired for it," he explains in that calm, dominant tone I adore. "You're perfectly normal. It's normal."

Normal. That's such a relief.

But there's more I need to say. "Derek?"

"Hmm?"

"I should tell you something."

His fingers still. "What is it, baby girl?"

"I was a virgin. Before you."

His body freezes. He moves me off his chest so he can look at me. "Why didn't you tell me?"

I'm instantly self-conscious. "I thought you wouldn't want me if you knew."

He drags a hand through his hair, jaw clenched. "Oh, I'd still want you. I just would've been more careful. Made it softer. Special."

"It was special," I say quickly, grabbing his hand. "It was exactly what I wanted."

He doesn't look convinced. "Evie, I had you spread out on your back on a picnic table. I almost didn't take you upstairs. That's not how your first time should have been."

"It's exactly how I wanted it," I say again, firmer. "It was hot. A little rough. And perfect."

His eyes soften for a moment and then cloud over. "Evie. Are you on birth control?"

There was never any reason to get on it with Todd since I didn't want to fuck him. My stomach drops. "No."

"Fuck." He sits up fast. "And we didn't use condoms. Jesus. What the hell was I thinking?"

I try to play it off. "It's probably fine. I mean, what are the odds I get knocked up the first time? Or...you know, the second."

His look shuts me up fast. "When's your period?"

I do the math. "Two weeks."

"Okay. We'll handle it if necessary, but I can't believe I was that careless."

"I'm sorry," I whisper as I sit up.

He cups my face, thumbs stroking my cheeks. "No, baby girl. This isn't on you. I'm the one with experience. I should've asked, made sure you were safe."

"So...what now?"

He exhales. "If this is going to continue—and I want it to— we're going to be smart. That starts with being careful. I'll use condoms from now on."

"But I want to feel you come inside me again." I blurt out before I can stop myself.

His eyes glitter. "You should be on birth control first. And we're both getting tested."

"But I was a virgin..."

"That doesn't matter. We do this right. I want you to see my clean results. And I want to see yours. It's about trust."

I feel the weight of his words. "Okay."

"Until then," he says firmly, "we wait. No risk. Got it?"

Every part of me wants to whine, but I keep it inside. "Deal."

He kisses me slower this time. Deep and sweet. Not rushed or ravenous—just...right. When he pulls back, I'm smiling. God, I want him again. I'm going to make that doctor appointment ASAP.

He raises a brow. "What's that smile for?"

"Just thinking how lucky I am to have run into you at that party. I had no idea how to even start exploring BDSM."

He stares at me intensely as if he can see deep into my soul. "I'm the lucky one, baby girl."

I curl back into his arms, safe and warm. This is perfect. No strings. No pressure. Just hot sex, deep trust, and all the kinky learning I can handle.

Okay, maybe the pregnancy scare part isn't ideal, but I'm not thinking about that. Not today.

He holds me tighter, and I sigh, boneless against him.

A sexy older man to dominate me and help me get over my loser ex? Yeah. This might be the smartest bad idea I've ever had.

CHAPTER 16

Derek

E vie's so fucking cute while at the same time unconsciously sexy that the thought of pushing her over the kitchen counter whenever we cook dinner together is a constant distraction. I've lost track of how many times I've had to redirect my thoughts as we do various mundane activities since our first night together. Everything seems torturous when I could be inside her with her heels behind my ass. Fuck, I'm a goner for her, and I begin to understand how it feels to slip into insanity.

I'm supposed to be the responsible adult, but over the last few days I've acted like a horny teenager. My struggle with the impulsive desire to fuck her on every flat surface is a living hell, but it's also calming to spend extended time with her. Despite the frustration of controlling my hormones, being around Evie is soothing, like I've smiled more the past few days. Even the guys at the shop look at me oddly when I walk out of my office whistling a tune. Is it just that I've had more sex lately, it's impossible to be grumpy after—Fuck, how many orgasms have I had?

Goddamn it, I've gotta stop fixating on our physical chemistry. I want to see what else there is between us; it's important.

Yet I continue to initiate prolonged necking on her couch in the living room, heavy petting on her tiny twin bed in her room, and fingering her until she's dancing on my fingertips as she comes apart. I have a near-permanent case of blue balls from the arousal of just being near her. But I can't get enough of her presence. I've practically moved in with her while her parents are on vacation. In the few short days since I made her mine, I've only been to my house to grab some clothes or start laundry.

She understood the importance of being responsible, getting an STI check, and a prescription for birth control. She decided on an implant, but she can't get it until we've confirmed she's not pregnant. In the interim, we'll have to use condoms. I bought two boxes of thirty-six, and a dozen pregnancy tests. I may have bought too many, but after using four condoms the day I brought them home and six more since, maybe I didn't buy enough.

Evie is upstairs taking a shower, and I'm downstairs flipping through my contacts and wiping out ancient hookups from my virtual little black book. If I was upstairs while she was naked, getting wet… There was a reason I purchased seventy-two condoms. Her phone buzzes on the coffee table, and I glance at the screen lighting up. We haven't gotten to the sharing passwords stage in our relationship, so I try to forget that the caller ID was from her doctor's office.

Why would a doctor call? Oh shit, maybe she's pregnant. Or has an STI. No, she was a virgin. But has she given a guy head? This only makes me remember how hot and tight she was when I fingered her draped over the picnic table in her backyard, then unknowingly took her virginity on her bed. Yep, now I want to rail her over the back of this couch. I close my eyes and think wholesome thoughts: apple pie, baseball bat, an ice cream sundae with a cherry on top, sucking on her tight hard nipples—*Fuck*. Before my mind spins out of control, she comes downstairs in her typical running shorts and nipples… I mean, tank top.

"You got a text," I say and tip my chin toward her phone.

"Thank you, sir," she says, kneeling beside me and tying her damp tresses into a ponytail. "I can read it later."

She licks her lips, then rubs her hands up my thighs, staring at me with a salacious gaze. I respond, or rather, my cock does, hardening quickly. I lower my eyes, tilting my head, and watching her curiously. I know what she's up to, but is she even going to include me in her plans?

"Something you want?" I ask lightly.

"Yes, sir," she says, then continues shamelessly. "Your cock in my mouth."

My dick pulses, and I want nothing more than to sink between her sinful lips.

"Is that how you ask?" I growl, dropping my phone to the side.

I glance at her fingers and lift a brow. Her forehead creases at my expression before she feigns innocence and pulls her hands behind her back. "Please, sir? May I suck your cock."

The impulse to rip my pants down and pull her pouty mouth into my groin is strong, but I force myself to be calm and slowly pry open my belt, then unsnap my jeans.

"You're such a needy cocksucker, aren't you?" I rumble low and rough, and I'm about to push my pants down to my knees when I spy her phone on the coffee table. I blink, then nod my chin. "Check your message first."

Part of what we've been discussing when we're not burning through my condom stash the past few days is how to be adults about things. I've set a poor example, fucking her at every opportunity like a hormone-addled teenager. I want this relationship to mean something, but fucking her at every turn may make her think she's just my fuck buddy.

I'm done with fuck buddies. I want to explore with her the heady power exchange in a dom-sub relationship. She said she wants to be trained, and that's what I'll do. I'll be the safe space for her to explore her fantasies—all of them. More than anything else, I want a relationship with Evie.

Evie pouts, and I want to reach out and grab her lower lip, pull her to me, kiss her as I haul her onto my lap, where she belongs. Instead, I pat my thighs. "I think it was your doctor. Do you want to read it together?"

She grabs her phone, and when she rises, I help her slide onto my lap. She chews on her lower lip as she wriggles into place, causing my shaft to throb. I tell it to be patient, but it's an asshole and stiffens instead, and I swallow a moan of pleasure. She glances at the phone, then up at me.

"Can I just peek first?" she asks, suddenly shy after begging to suck my cock moments ago.

"Sure." I nod, even though I want us to read it together. I pull her back against my chest, her legs draped over my thighs. I kiss her temple and force myself to look at anything except her screen.

"STI panel is clean." She pushes her phone at me and curls her body into mine. "I told you so!"

Exhaling, I wrap my arms around her and squeeze tight. Kissing her temple again, I notice her glance up at me as she shifts her hips, rocking against my erection.

"Babe, I *knew* you were clean. But we're being responsible adults, right?"

"Right." She tilts her head. "I'm sorry, Derek. This is good news, though. Right?"

"The best," I agree.

She purses her lips, tapping that tempting plump bottom bow with her fingernail. "Should I call the clinic and make an appointment for the implant?"

I grin at her and nod, and she leans back against my shoulder as she dials, then stares at the ceiling as it rings. I can't help cupping and squeezing her pert boob, and she giggles. Then, she sits up and listens. I continue to lightly tickle her as she has a conversation with the nurse, making her squirm in my lap, which only makes my cock harden.

"Thank you," she says, and I tune in to her words as she slides the phone back onto the coffee table.

"Ugh, they told me to call back when my period starts." She frowns.

"It's a good thing I bought so many condoms." I grin to show her that there is a bright side to the story.

She wriggles again before hopping off to sashay toward the stairs. She pauses at the first step, then pushes her gym shorts down and kicks them off. She stares at me while I enjoy a tour of her amazing legs, then pulls off her tank and tosses it toward me. The vixen is shamelessly naked as she smirks at me and keeps walking up to her room.

I twist off the couch, leaving my phone on the cushion, and chase after her. I know I pre-staged a dozen condoms by her bed, there should be a few left. My cock aches in my jeans as I hurry, losing my cool as I anticipate sinking my shaft into her tight pussy. I'm a fucking goner. Refusing her is impossible, but I shouldn't let her know how tightly I'm wound around her finger. I force myself to slow down and purposefully land on each step before I hit the landing and stroll to her room.

CHAPTER 17

Eve

My heart pounds as I bolt for my bedroom, Derek right behind me. I throw myself onto the bed and spread my legs wide, grinning as the cool air hits my slick heat.

When he gets to the room and stops cold, his eyes rake over me like I'm the only thing he wants to devour. His stare lingers on my tits, then lower—to where I'm wet and aching for him. The bulge in his jeans is huge.

Five minutes ago, I was begging for his cock in my mouth. Now, the hunger is different—more desperate. I need him inside me.

"You're playing with fire," he rumbles.

Without thinking, I trail a finger down my belly, stopping just above my pussy. The words tumble out before I can second-guess them. "I want you to breed me. Fill me with your cum."

The second I hear myself, my cheeks flame, but it's too late to take it back.

His eyes flare so intensely it feels like the air between us crackles. "You want that, huh?"

I drag my fingers between my folds, circling my clit. "Mmm, yes. I want to feel you come deep inside me."

He pulls open the nightstand drawer. "You know that's not happening tonight, baby girl."

I pout as he tears open the condom packet and rolls it down his thick cock. "A girl can dream, can't she?"

He climbs onto the bed and grips my waist, pulling me right where he wants me.

"You want me to fill you up, huh? Pump you so full of cum you're dripping for days?"

"God, yes. Please. Fill me."

He rubs the tip of his cock along my pussy, teasing me, not pushing in. "Tell me. Say it."

I tremble. "I want your cum. I want to feel it flooding into me. I want you to breed me."

He crashes his mouth into mine, kissing me like he owns me. And then—finally—he sinks inside.

I cry out as he stretches me open, his cock thick and perfect, dragging along every nerve ending.

"Fuck, you feel amazing," he groans, thrusting in slow, steady strokes.

"Harder. Please," I pant, clutching his shoulders as I grind up into him.

His pace turns feral, hips slamming into me. "I'm going to fuck you full of cum. Tie you to this bed and use you until you're leaking all over the sheets."

That image—me, bound and wrecked, dripping with him— makes me explode.

"Oooh, god!" My orgasm rips through me and I cry out, body clenching around him.

He doesn't stop, and just keeps pounding into me as I babble, "I want to be your slut. Tie me up. Spank me. Use me."

His groan is guttural. "You're my greedy little cumslut, baby girl."

He pulls out, flips me over, and I barely manage to lift my ass before he's inside me again, deeper this time.

He grabs my ponytail and yanks my head back. The stretch, the control, the angle—it's overwhelming.

"So good," I moan, mouth open, drooling onto the sheets.

He fucks me faster, and I meet every thrust, pushing back like a cock-drunk mess.

"Fuck, Evie," he growls.

And just like that, the filthiest fantasy hits me—I'm already pregnant, round and full, and he's still fucking me from behind, claiming me.

My orgasm hits like a shockwave. "Oooh, fuck!" I scream, slamming back onto him. "Breed me. Please, fill me with cum."

He lets go of my hair and digs his fingers into my hips, rutting into me like an animal. I lower my head to the mattress, moaning and sobbing as another orgasm slams through me.

With a groan, Derek tenses and slams into me one final time, shuddering with his climax. I imagine he's really filling me.

He pulls out slowly, and I collapse onto the bed, giggling. I'm dizzy with satisfaction.

He stretches out beside me and rubs my back, soothing me as I float. Having a dom is better than I ever imagined.

Still, a part of me can't stop thinking about how turned on I got at the thought of being pregnant. I shouldn't want that. Not really. But...maybe I do?

I melt into him as he pulls me close, but the moment is broken by his ringtone blaring from downstairs. It's playing the oldies song "Hot for Teacher."

Oh jeez. "Seriously? Who even listens to that anymore? Are you secretly ancient?"

He smacks my ass. "Watch it, baby girl. Keep teasing me and I'll redden that ass again and make you apologize."

My pussy clenches, but I'm too boneless to act on it.

The phone keeps ringing.

Derek sighs and peels away from me. "Might be work."

He heads downstairs, and a small frown crosses my face, already missing his warmth.

A few minutes later, he returns with an apologetic look. "Gotta run. Computer glitch at the shop."

"Do you have to?" I give him a pleading look.

He leans in and kisses me. "I'll call you later, all right?"

"Okay, Sir," I say sweetly. The honorific makes my pussy twitch all over again.

Once he's gone, I roll onto my back, still throbbing from everything he just did to me. God, no one's ever made me feel like this.

But reality starts creeping in. Three days. That's all I have before my parents come back. And then what? We can't keep fucking under their roof. I'll have to remind him to get his stuff out of the house.

I hug a pillow to my chest and let myself drift. I imagine his apartment. Curling up on his couch. Cooking for him. Sitting in his lap while he calls me 'baby girl.'

Wait. What am I doing? This is supposed to be just sex. A hot little dom/sub fling with no commitment.

So why does it feel like more?

I sit up, heart pounding, frustration simmering. I will *not* be that girl. The one who confuses orgasms for love. Who melts at a sweet name and starts imagining futures.

No.

This is just sex.

Mind-blowing, filthy, perfect sex.

I shove the thoughts away and force myself to breathe. He gives me what I want. No promises. No complications.

And that's enough. Right?

...Right?

CHAPTER 18
Derek

Evie is pressing every single one of my buttons. She's found them all and now is intent on driving me fucking crazy with each seemingly innocent move and touch. She might be inexperienced in the bedroom, but she's got plenty of natural talent on how to be a seductress. She's learning to take me deep in her mouth like a champ, always wanting to see how much of me she can take. That eager determination in her eyes when she's on her knees makes it almost impossible to maintain my control. It doesn't help that whenever we're together, she practically throws herself at me, pleading for me to fuck her —to breed her. Jesus—we still don't know if I knocked her up that first night, and she's begging for my cum. But I'm not risking that—my cock just has to get used to its latex prison for now.

But damn, she has such a sexy little body and a sweet ass that I could eat up, leaving teeth marks and claiming her as mine. Her big, expressive eyes stare at me with trust and innocence even as she preens for me. I can't keep my eyes off her tight curves which spark an ongoing movie in my head of all the unmentionable things I want to do with her. She's the most tempting thing I've ever experienced.

If Evie weren't a submissive little treasure who I want to train and teach, I'd have her bent over a counter with her panties down, getting fucked right now. But instead, we're in a booth sitting across from each other in a restaurant surrounded by other diners because I'm committed to making this more than just fucking. She might not know it, but I want her. All of her.

Tonight is the third date away from her house or mine. Our previous two dates have been dinner, movies, and long, drawn-out conversations about life, but not about sex, not even after we left. Even if we end up with her snuggled in my arms, half-asleep on my couch or her bed. I know I'm torturing myself, but the time alone with her is perfect, and I can't resist spending the night with her cuddled up to me.

I'm becoming addicted to her. It doesn't help that every morning, I wake up hard and aching, wishing I had fucked her to sleep the night before. But I'm taking this time to get to know her better. It's worth it. I've learned more about her, and she is discovering me, too. She's curious about my business and how I run it. She's stopped by the shop a few times and just watched me work with my team to serve our customers. She might just want to be near me, hoping I'll drag her into my office, close the blinds, brush everything onto the floor, spread her nubile body across my desk, and fuck her hard until I blast my load deep inside her.

Fuck.

I shut my eyes, attempting to purge my thoughts of that enticing picture, but it's only for a moment before they snap back open because I'm hooked on watching her pretty face sitting across the table.

As if sensing my thoughts, Evie gives me a sultry grin that makes me shift in my seat, trying to find a comfortable position.

When she notices, her smile widens, and she bats her eyelashes. "Is something wrong?"

Damn this woman, but I can't be mad at her, not when she wriggles and makes her boobs bounce, while grinning so cutely. "Baby girl, are you done? We can leave."

Evie pushes her plate to the side, but instead of leaving the table, she leans forward, giving me an eyeful of her delectable cleavage. She's wearing a cute, white summer dress with small, bright pink flowers printed on it, and a scoop neck showing off her tits perfectly. "What now?"

"Movie?" I suggest. We haven't picked anything yet, and maybe we'll wind up seeing a terrible movie and spend most of the show making out.

"I have a better idea," she announces, leaning back into the booth. I feel her bare foot inching up my leg towards my crotch.

I'm instantly rock hard and arch one eyebrow. "What're you doing?"

She bites her lip adorably, seemingly innocent yet so incredibly sexy that I'm tempted to haul her across the table and fuck her on her knees in front of the other customers as she cries out. Instead, I put a hand on her ankle, holding her still, trying to flag down the waitress. I've gotta pay and get her out of here. She wiggles her toes, distracting me by how close they are to my cock. The room is warm, and I let go of her ankle to take a sip of water to cool down as she continues. Finally, I get the attention of a waitress, and she approaches our table.

"So, my better idea," Evie purrs. "Why don't you take me back to your place and breed me?"

I almost spit up my water, coughing to clear my throat and struggling to breathe as her foot makes contact with my cock.

I gasp, unable to speak, while the waitress asks, "Will there be anything else?"

Fuck. I shake my head while studying Evie. She smiles innocently, as if her foot isn't currently rubbing against my erection and she wasn't just talking about me pumping her full of my cum with the waitress hovering right beside us. I settle the bill waving my phone at the device she's holding.

Once we're alone again, I take hold of Evie's foot. "Baby girl." I growl my best warning tone to show she's misbehaving.

Eve smirks, leans her elbows on the table, and rests her chin on her hands, gazing at me with wide-eyed adoration. "Mmm, yes? Is there a problem?"

Jesus Christ, this woman is going to be the death of me. I'm trying not to groan. "Don't start something you can't finish."

"Oh." Evie pouts, sticking her bottom lip out at me. "You mean you aren't taking me home to breed me?"

It's official. I've found my own personal hell, and I'm stuck here with her torturing me for eternity with no escape. Not that I want to. After paying, I help her stand while she slips her high heels back on. I escort her to the car, relieved that at least if we're sitting next to each other driving, she can't distract me.

On the way back, Evie chatters happily about everything: her job hunt, the movie trailer she saw online the day before, and her new favorite music band. I love her enthusiasm for life and her passion for all the little details. It feels like we're growing closer beyond her just tempting and teasing me. After leaving the restaurant, she is more animated than usual, and I keep drifting back to her comment.

"Did you mean it?"

"Mean what?" Evie feigns confusion.

I peek over at her before returning to the road again. "About me breeding you."

Evie giggles and shifts, moving her dress up her legs so the hem is just below her pussy. I glance down, and a jolt runs through me when she reveals she's not wearing any panties. Fuck, this woman is a temptation beyond my limits.

"Oh, about breeding this?" Evis asks, soft and playful.

When her fingers slide between her legs, and she begins to play with herself, a thrill shoots through me. The only thing keeping me from pulling the car over is the traffic. If there were no other cars around and we weren't on the highway, I'd be fucking her by now.

As it is, I'm stuck, listening to her moan while I keep driving.

Our windows are down, and when a truck passes us on the left, the breeze ruffles the neckline of her dress. It's blown aside, exposing the tops of her breasts, her erect nipples tenting the light material. I can't stop myself. I glance at her again before turning back to the road and growling, "If you're not careful, I'll pull over and fuck you in this car."

"Oh!" Evie's hand stops moving, and I can feel her staring at me, as if she's unsure whether I'm teasing. After a few moments, she gives me a shy smile and whispers, "Would that be bad?"

There's no way this is happening. There is not a chance in hell that I'll have sex with her while driving on the highway. Nope, not going to happen. "Baby girl, I don't want to spend a night in jail for indecent exposure, and what I'd do to you would be *extremely* indecent."

When I glance at her again, and her eyes light up as she squirms in her seat and licks her lips, I know I've lost. I can't resist the temptation she presents.

Evie moves her hand between her legs again, and I fantasize about how soft and wet she'd feel wrapped around my stiff shaft. Barely audible above the sound of the engine and the wind blowing through the window Evie asks, "What would you do to me?"

As a semi roars by, blasting us with its draft, ruffling the top of her dress again, revealing more of her tits, she moans and closes her eyes. Hot damn, she's so fucking sexy. I want her. Right now. In this car, in a parking lot, wherever I can.

We're almost back at her house, but as soon as I pull off the exit ramp, I search for a quiet spot to park and make her mine again.

Evie's panting, and her hips are writhing as she pleasures herself, and I can barely drive.

"You're being a naughty girl."

When she continues to rub her clit, her breathing gets louder, and she moans. "Yes, so naughty."

"Did you ask permission to play with yourself?"

A shiver of excitement runs through me. There's nothing like an obedient submissive, and Eve is the perfect mix of naughty, bratty, and nice, which is a turn-on that's beyond anything I've ever known. I have to have her. "Naughty girls deserve punishment."

A whimper escapes her lips before she tosses her head back, her mouth falling open. Her eyes are filled with pleasure, and darkening, wanting something more. I know what she requires. Me.

As I drive down the street, watching for a safe, isolated spot, I sense Evie continuing to play with her slick pussy. She's egging me on, tempting me with her soft moans and the wet sounds her fingers make. I've learned what each of her sighs means, and it's too much. I want her. Now. We skid to a stop under a broken streetlight in the farthest corner of a deserted parking lot. The car sways from the suddenness, and Evie arches her back, rolling her head toward me with lust in her eyes.

In a quick motion, I undo my belt and unzip my pants and push them down along with my boxers, releasing my cock, and stroke myself, feeling the slickness of pre-cum coating my crown. I have the presence of mind to grab a condom from my back pocket and sheathe myself. Evie watches me roll it down my length with wide eyes, and her hand is still playing with her clit, as her breathing grows faster.

I can't take any more of this and open the car door. "Get out."

She immediately obeys, climbing out her side as I stalk my prey around the car, pulling her into me when she's within reach. Her arms circle my neck, and she holds on to me as I lift her up and set her tight ass down on the car's hood. My loose jeans slip down to my knees, and my cock throbs, jutting out as she spreads her thighs.

I push her skirt out of the way, and she moans and wraps her legs around me as I sink into her depths. I let out an indulgent moan as her silky warmth envelops me. My brain shuts off, and I'm consumed with the urge to fuck her hard.

My lizard brain takes over, and I slam into her wildly, gripping her thighs and pulling her into my firm thrusts. I'm feral as I lock into her wanton gaze, driving my cock into her like a rutting beast. When her hands clutch my shirt and her legs tighten around my hips, I know she's desperate. "Daddy, please, I'm so close. Breed me."

That's all it takes. I drive my cock into her tight pussy with fervent want. Her breathless moans and peeps of pleasure are all encouraging my possessive depravity. I kiss her savagely, devouring her mouth and staking my claim on her body and soul. It's primal, rough, and just what our bodies crave as we crash together.

She breaks off the kiss, crying out loudly as her pussy spasms. Her body shakes—legs tightening, pulling me deeper as I watch her come apart. With a roar of triumph, I empty myself inside her—hips jerking as I pump shot after shot into the rubber prison. My ass tightens, jerking with every thrust and thinking I'm flooding her fertile womb with my cum. The world fades away, leaving us alone in the darkness and silence, connected in a way that I can only describe with two words.

She's mine.

When an icy breeze blows against my damp skin, reality slowly returns. I realize we're parked under a busted street light tucked into an abandoned parking lot's dark and filthy corner.

When Eve shivers, I pull her off the hood and into my arms and carry her to the passenger seat, waddling with my jeans around my ankles. Once she's inside, I pull my jeans up over my ass and hurry around to the driver's side, climbing in awkwardly and sitting as I carefully pull off the condom. I drop it in the trash bag hanging off the dash, bridge. I leave my fly unbuttoned, as I slide in the key, slam the door, and start the engine.

The car roars to life, and I twist the heat to max, then glance at her to ensure she is settled and the windows are closed. I pull her across the dividing console into my lap, wrapping my arms around her for a deep kiss. I brush her hair out of her face. "Baby girl, are you okay?"

Eve's soft sleepy nod as her heavy eyelids close, comfort me before she smiles. "That was so hot."

I chuckle. That's not the word I would have used—'mind-blowing' or 'life-altering' seem more apropos. My practical side knows it was a risk that could have gotten both of us in trouble if a cop had driven past. I have no regrets. I had to show her what she does to me. Immediately, right here in this crusty old parking lot.

"Come on, let's go home."

With a sigh, Eve turns and crawls over the console and back into the passenger seat. When she's comfortable, I reach across her to pull the seat belt around her hips. As I put the car in gear she slumps over the divider to rest her head against my arm and closes her eyes.

As I drive, I wonder if she understands she's mine. Not just something to say in the heat of the moment, but that I possess her. I'm never giving her up. Ever. It's not just her body that I want—it's how I feel around her. She brightens my world and makes me relax and enjoy life. Her enthusiasm and willingness to experiment and learn are impressive. She's everything I want in a partner, and I don't care that she's my best friend's sister. I'd risk my future to be with her.

There's no way she could know how deeply and ultimately I've fallen for her because I haven't told her—not yet, but I will soon.

CHAPTER 19
Eve

My heart lurches when we pull up in front of the house and I see an unfamiliar car in the driveway. My parents. They're home.

They're getting out of an Uber, dragging their luggage behind them. Shit. I wasn't ready for this yet. Not the hiding. Not the pretending. After everything with Derek, going back to their rules of telling them where I'm going and when I'll be back feels suffocating.

Before Derek can kill the ignition, I twist toward him. "I'm getting out before they see you."

His jaw tightens. "Are you going to tell your parents about us?"

"At some point."

Tell them what—that their daughter has been getting spanked and fucked senseless by their son's best friend?

His disapproval hits me like a slap. "Sooner or later, you'll have to. And the longer you delay, the harder it'll be."

"Okay."

I don't want to admit the truth—I'm afraid he'll be long gone by the time it even matters.

"Wait, what does that mean?" Derek scowls. "Are you going to tell them?"

I falter, unwilling to commit to a timeframe. "Yeah, I'll tell them...soon."

"Fine." He lets out a frustrated grunt.

Seriously? What's the rush? Cole told me to wait until we're married. And Derek? He's not the forever type.

"You don't know my parents—"

He cuts me off with a dry laugh. "Baby, I know your parents. I'm Cole's best friend, remember? I've known them for half your life."

Ugh. Right.

"I said I'll tell them. Just give me time."

Out of the corner of my eye, I see my mom waving and heading toward the car—oh god. "I need to go."

I freeze when his hand closes on my thigh, and he says, "I'm not fucking you again until you tell them. They're going to have to get used to us being together. I'm not going anywhere."

I stare at him, stunned. What the hell is happening? Since when are we *a thing* he wants people to get used to?

"Go."

I scramble out of the car, pulse racing. My mom greets me and gives a long look at Derek's car as he drives away before she drags me inside, chirping about their trip. Thank god, I don't think she realized who I was with. I listen to her and pretend everything's fine, but my head is spinning.

The moment I get free, I rush upstairs and collapse onto my bed. What the fuck was that? Derek laying down an ultimatum like we're some kind of couple. Isn't this just sex?

Okay, yes, sex so good it breaks my brain. But still, that doesn't mean we have a future. And Cole told me not to tell Mom and Dad unless I was walking down the aisle, so now we have to hide it again. Lie. Sneak around. Make excuses. It's going to be hell.

I grab my phone and dial the one person who might talk some sense into me.

Andrea picks up after a few rings. "Hey, what's up?"

"I need help."

I hear a door close on her end. "Okay, I'm alone. Spill."

"What do I do about Derek?"

She goes silent for a moment. "Wait. Derek as in *Cole's best friend* Derek?"

I wince. "Yeah...so after the party and the whole ice thing—wait. Why haven't you been texting me?"

"Been busy. But whatever, this is about you. Talk."

God, where do I even start? "It was amazing. Like, *best night of my life* amazing."

She squeals, and I roll my eyes, but I can't help smiling.

"Okay," she says, breathless. "Back up. What does that have to do with Derek?"

"He fucked me."

"Shut up!" she screeches. "You slept with Derek? How was it?"

"So good. So, so good." I blush as I think back. God, that really was amazing.

"Holy shit."

I take a breath. "And then Cole found out."

"Cole *knows*?"

"He walked in the next morning while we were making breakfast. Derek had me up on the counter and I was about ready to beg him to fuck me."

"When was this?"

I wave a hand like she can see me. "I don't know, a week ago?"

Andrea snorts. "Or more like ten days?"

Why is she being weird? Who cares? "That's not the point.

The point is Cole knows, and now Derek won't fuck me again until I tell my parents."

That distracts her. "Wait. He *actually* said that?"

"Yep. Like it's some line in the sand."

I fill her in on everything—the sex on the car, the spanking, the picnic table. The way he keeps checking in, telling me to talk to him, saying we should take it slow. But then still bending me over and fucking me roughly like he can't help himself.

When I finally finish, she exhales. "Eve, it sounds like Derek likes you."

My heart jumps. "You're joking."

She doesn't answer, and in that silence, every possible future rushes through my mind. Him leaving. Getting bored. Breaking me. Me crying like some lovesick idiot.

Andrea finally speaks. "I wouldn't joke about this. Everything you just described? That's a man who *likes* you. Like, *likes you*-likes you. You should talk to him."

Sure. Easy. I'll just casually ask, "Hey, are you into me or just trying to get your dick sucked?"

But before I can say anything, Andrea's voice rushes through the speaker. "Crap, I have to go. Just talk to him, okay?"

The call ends.

I drop my phone beside me. Andrea thinks he likes me. God, I hope she's right.

I get ready for bed in a daze. As I brush my teeth, the conversation with Derek loops through my brain. The way he looked at me when I tried to slink out of his car. His ultimatum. How knowing he's unhappy makes me wish I could go back in time and say something else in the car when he told me to tell my parents about us.

And then it hits me—a clarity so sudden and obvious that I actually stop with my toothbrush still in my mouth. The racing pulse whenever he's close. The way I can't stop thinking about him. The constant pull toward him that I've been fighting.

I'm in love with Derek.

The realization washes over me and I close my eyes as everything clicks into place. It's not just an attraction or lust or even a crush. I'm completely, utterly in love with him.

I'm not sure what tomorrow will bring, but I know one thing for sure:

I need to talk to Derek. As soon as I can.

CHAPTER 20
Derek

Pushing the door open, I throw my keys across my living room. They smack into the back of the sofa, then fall behind the cushion. Fuck. I hang my head and slowly close the door.

I'm on edge. Angry. Mostly at myself, but for fuck's sake, Evie —read the room. I won't stop or slow down because your parents are home. That isn't what this is about. I'm not going to sneak around under her parents' noses. I respect them too much, and that she doesn't see that makes my guts clench.

This isn't a fucking game.

I sink onto the sofa, plunging my hand behind the cushion and touching the keys. They fall all the way through and clatter to the floor. What the fuck. I twist around, tossing the cushions across the room. Then, grab the sofa and yank it away from the wall. A leg hits the keys, and I hear them clatter across the floor.

What the ever-loving fuck!

I walk to the kitchen, whipping open the refrigerator door, and see my choices: bottle of beer or flat soda. I squeeze my eyes shut, grab the two-liter bottle, twist off the top, and guzzle from the half-full container.

I'd usually grab the six-pack and have a little pity party of one, watching porn, but I'm done with drinking away my worries. It never helped. I want to be a better person because of her—Evie. The scared girl that is afraid to tell her parents about me.

Shit.

I take another swig of the flat soda before walking back into the living room. I carefully lift the couch, snag my errant keys, then walk back to the front door and put them in the little dish with my wallet. Combing my fingers through my hair, I drain the rest of the soda before exhaling a long breath.

Fuck, okay. What now?

I deposit the empty bottle in the kitchen recycling bin, return to the living room, reposition the sofa, arrange the cushions neatly, and then turn and sit down. Grabbing the remote, I flick on the TV, closing my eyes while it starts up. I have to wait for my streaming box to boot up, and I take that moment to inventory my night.

Date with Evie at the restaurant—check.

Sex with Evie in a dark parking lot—check.

Telling her folks about us—big. Fat. ZERO.

Why do I care? I've had plenty of girlfriends and submissives. I've never even seen their parents, much less known their names. I've known Janice and Pete since I was in college. Cole has invited me to fucking holiday family celebrations multiple times. They're great people, and they'd understand. Not because they think I'm perfect, but because they love their daughter.

That stops my thought train.

Fuck.

I love her. It's not just possessive ownership dom bullshit, or my crazy feelings. I love her, I want to protect her.

What the fuck am I supposed to do with that?

I've never been in love. I'm a fuck 'em and leave 'em asshole. Except I haven't had one thought of ditching Evie since the night of the barbecue, where Cole left me alone with his little sister.

Holy fuck. I love my best friend's sister.

Now I'm rethinking the beer in the fridge. I should call Cole. He's my best friend; he may have some advice.

Fuck. No. He's the last person I should call.

I shove my hand into my pocket and grab my phone. This won't take long, so I swipe and glance at the screen so it unlocks, my battery is at 1%. I flick my thumb to the contacts list. Who can I talk to about a fucking relationship? I stab at Jasper's name and hold it to my ear.

"Derek," Jasper rasps. "Do you fucking know what time it is?"

What time is it? I pull the phone from my ear and stare at the screen. 11:39 pm. Fuck.

"Sorry, man, I can call you back in the morning."

"You're already on the line," Jasper says, and I hear a whisper on his end.

"You have someone over, man. I'll call back."

"She was just leaving," he says. "It's cool; she's aftercared out."

"Okay." I don't know what to say to that.

"She gets antsy when I get cuddly."

The picture of Jasper getting cuddly makes me snort-laugh.

"Hey man, I need it too. Don't be a dick. Now why are you calling me when it's damn near tomorrow?"

"I... Fuck."

"I'm good, thanks," Jasper drawls, then laughs.

"I think I'm in love."

"And?"

"What am I supposed to do about that?"

"Fuck if I know, I'm twice divorced. I thought I was in love once."

"What happened?"

"You know I used to be a raging alcoholic, right? Did time in the joint for aggravated assault. Dude—*I'm* what happened. How about you not follow my fucking example?"

"Sorry," I say and huff out a breath. "I'll figure it out. Sorry to bother you."

"Derek." Jasper softens before then breaks out his 'don't fuck with me', command. "You love her, Derek. That's what you do. You do everything possible to show her you have her. You hear me?

"It's Evelyn."

Jasper grunts. "You know I'm her neighbor, right? You two haven't been exactly stealthy."

"Her parents just got back," I confess, scratching my head. "She didn't want me around, and now."

"What?"

"I don't want to lose her, but I gotta know she's all in. I am."

"Her parents aren't the problem," Jasper yawns. "Pete will overreact then slowly accept you're better for her than the other assholes around town. If Janice sees what I see when Evelyn looks at you, she'll side with her."

"So what do I do about Evie?"

Jasper chuckles. "Evie, huh? Yeah. That tracks. Okay, this is what you do. You show up. Every. Time. She'll come around."

"How do you know?" I curse under my breath. "What if she doesn't love me...What if she drops me? Fuck."

"Derek. It's late, not the best time to overthink things. Get some sleep, and see what happens in the morning. Jesus fuck, kid. Take a fucking brea—."

The line drops, and I blink at the blank screen. Fucking great, it's dead.

I stand and go to my room. My bed is empty. The fact that I haven't slept alone since the barbecue clangs around in my head. Of course, Jasper saw me there.

Dropping my phone on the magnetic charger, I strip, pull on my pajama pants, and climb into bed. The sheets are like ice. Okay, they aren't icy, but they're not the heat of Evie I've grown used to.

I stare at the ceiling for a long time before the darkness takes me.

CHAPTER 21

Eve

The moment I wake up, I know exactly what I'm going to do. No more waiting. No more hiding.

After I shower and fix my hair, I slip into my favorite floral dress and pack an overnight bag—just in case. I hurry downstairs, hoping my parents are around. I want to do this face-to-face. Together. This is something I only want to say once.

They're both in the living room. Mom has a cup of coffee and is scrolling through her phone, while Dad is watching the giant television in his recliner.

They look up, surprised.

I plant my bag by the door and square my shoulders. "Mom. Dad. Can we talk?"

Mom sets her mug down, and Dad clicks the remote, silencing the TV.

Deep breath. "I've been spending a lot of time with Derek."

Mom frowns, processing. "Cole's Derek?"

"No. *My* Derek."

Her brow tightens. "Your Derek used to be Cole's Derek. Right?"

"Yeah. Not anymore."

Dad's face hardens, and he sits forward. "What's changed?"

"We're...seeing each other."

They're quiet. Did I shock them? My pulse races. "We're dating. And we've had sex. Last night. On the hood of his car. In a parking lot."

A beat of stunned silence.

Dad jerks back like I smacked him. "Jesus Christ, Eve!" he thunders. "Are you kidding me right now? He's your brother's best friend. And so much older than you. He's—he's like family!"

My stomach drops. I expected some resistance, but the raw anger in Dad's voice makes my blood run cold. This isn't the slightly uncomfortable but ultimately accepting reaction I'd hoped for.

Mom's eyes widen and she presses her hand against her breastbone. "Eve..." The disappointment in her voice cuts through me like a knife. I can see it in her eyes—she thinks I've made a terrible mistake.

Dad shoves off the couch, pacing like a man possessed. "That son of a bitch." His eyes cut toward the door. "This isn't right. I'm going over to his place right now."

"Dad!" Panic claws up my throat. Oh god, what have I done? This is so much worse than I imagined.

Mom stands and grabs his arm, holding him in place. "Pete, no. Not like this. Getting in his face won't help anything."

Dad's chest is rising and falling like he's just sprinted a mile. "He took advantage of her, Janice. She's just a kid."

I feel sick. They're acting like I'm sixteen, not twenty-four. Like I'm some victim Derek preyed on. The shock morphs into indignation.

"I'm not a kid!" My voice breaks, full of tears and fury. "I love him."

Dad's jaw tightens and Mom's expression flickers, her

concern warring with reluctant understanding. "Eve, are you sure? This isn't just...leftover feelings from Todd?"

"No." I feel steel in my spine as I face them. "It's not a mistake. I love him. And he loves me."

Dad huffs. "Love's not supposed to start on the hood of a car."

"No, it started before that," I fire back. "While you were on vacation."

For a moment, no one speaks. The tension pulls so tight I can barely breathe.

Finally, Mom's shoulders drop. She releases Dad's arm and steps closer to me. "If you're serious about this, if you truly believe this is real, then we'll deal with it. But Eve, this path won't be easy. People will judge you. Even your brother."

"I know," I whisper, not mentioning that Cole is well aware I'm with Derek. "I don't care."

Dad's still fuming but at least he's not storming out the door. "You should care," he grumbles, but I can tell he's lost some of his outrage.

Mom picks up my bag and hands it to me as she walks with me out the door. Out of earshot of Dad, she gives me a worried look. "Just promise me something?"

"Anything."

"Promise me you won't let him break your heart like Todd did."

"I'll try." A lump forms in my throat, and I throw my arms around her, hugging her tight. "Thanks, Mom. I'll text you if I'm not coming home tonight."

She hugs me back, holding on longer than I expect. When she pulls away, there's still fear in her eyes—but also pride.

"He better treat you right."

"He will," I promise, and squeeze her hand before heading to the car.

Once I'm in the driver's seat, a goofy grin spreads across my face. I'm tempted to text him to warn him I'm coming, but resist. When I show up, I'm going to jump him and not let him escape until we've talked and fucked. That should work. Right?

When I arrive at Derek's apartment, I knock but he doesn't come to the door. I try the doorknob, but it's locked.

Fuck. Where did he go? I try calling him, but he doesn't answer, so I dial Cole instead.

He sounds friendly as he greets me. "Hey, Eve."

"Hi." I hesitate for a moment. "Do you know where Derek is?"

Cole seems puzzled. "Nope."

Double fuck. Where is he, and why did he disappear? Is this some sort of punishment or payback?

I ask Cole, "Can you please call him and have him call me?"

After a pause, he agrees. "Sure, I'll do that, but I'm meeting up with someone in an hour, so I might not hear from him until later."

Ugh, shit. "That's fine. Just whatever you can do. Thanks!"

As I end the call, an apartment door down the hall opens, and I hear Derek's laughter mixed with a woman's voice I don't recognize. My heart plummets to my stomach as Derek walks out, wearing pajama pants and a T-shirt.

Her flirty reply doesn't help my panic. "Thank you for every-thing, Derek."

She closes the door, and when he turns to walk to his apart-ment, he notices me. He freezes. "Evie."

Shit, this looks bad, and my gut twists as the woman's words to him replays in my head. I'm reminded of catching Todd fucking my roommate. I can't go through this again.

Derek's speech is cautious but not hostile. "Did you just get here?"

"Yes."

A shadow crosses his face. I can see a hint of panic. "Her sink was clogged and overflowing. I helped her turn the water off so she could call the landlord."

As he unlocks his door, he gives me a concerned look and steps back to hold the door open. "Are you coming inside?"

I enter his apartment and the air feels denser as the door closes behind us. When Derek touches my arm, I can feel his warmth. My brain clears, and my tension eases. Derek isn't Todd, and when I caught Todd cheating, he blamed me. He didn't respond the same way Derek is right now. Todd didn't care about me, Derek does.

I love him. He's not playing games, and he's not a liar. I woke up this morning knowing it was time to be honest and talk things through with Derek—to act like a grown-up who's worthy of having a deeper relationship with him.

"I've been an idiot," I blurt out.

Derek says nothing and his face remains calm while he caresses my arm lightly.

I murmur, "I thought you just wanted to fuck me and weren't serious about me."

"No." Derek pulls me closer to him, and his lips brush against my forehead before trailing down to the tip of my nose. "I want more than that." When he finally kisses me, a thrill runs from my fingertips to my toes, and I'm unable to resist melting against his body and savoring the touch, taste, and smell of him.

When his hands slide down and cup my ass, pulling me into his hips, his erection is obvious, and my pussy throbs with desire.

Breaking off the kiss, I'm left panting. "So you want to be my boyfriend and not just my dom?"

"Phrase it however you want. You're mine, Evie."

He gazes at me with adoration and passion as the heat in my core intensifies.

"Do you understand what that means?" he asks.

Holy fuck, it means so many things. So, so many hot, delicious, dirty, and exciting things.

As my knees grow weak, Derek holds me tight. When his lips brush against mine again, I'm already lost in a haze of pleasure and barely register his next question.

"Who do you belong to?"

"You."

"Good girl." Derek's smile is warm and approving. "And who do I belong to?"

That one is easy. "Me."

Derek kisses me deeply, and when his tongue slides into my mouth, exploring and claiming me, his grip on my ass is firm. He does own me, and is always going to take care of me, and we're a team, regardless of the circumstances.

Derek pulls back from me, and I whimper in dissatisfaction. I thought that was going well.

"Baby girl, I meant it when I said I wouldn't fuck you until you spoke to your parents."

My insides simmer with pleasure, and I arch an eyebrow at him. "Oh?"

"Yes." He moves across the room, putting distance between us.

I toe my shoes off and pull my dress over my head, revealing a matching blue lace panty and bra set. I sway my hips and this time he's my prey I'm stalking instead of the other way around. He gives a quick glance around, like he's trying to plan his escape.

"I think you're going to fuck me right here, right now."

Derek groans. "Baby—"

When I get close enough, his hand brushes against my shoulder as if he's going to stop me from pressing against him. I push his hand away and drop to my knees in front of him, gazing at his crotch. There's a distinct tenting of his loose pajama pants, and he's ready to fill my mouth, and possibly my pussy.

When I run a finger along his bulge, Derek moans, and I know I've won.

"I can't resist you." He says with deep tenderness as he threads his fingers through my hair.

I pull his pants down, freeing his cock, and I want to hum in happiness. I stroke him slowly, looking up at him so I can watch his pleasure.

I place a kiss on the tip of his cock and I giggle when it pulses in my hand.

"Oh, by the way—" I keep my tone casual on purpose. "Before I left, I told my parents we're dating, and they're fine with it...or will be after they get over the shock of hearing you defiled me on the hood of your car."

He lets out a strangled laugh. "You didn't."

I make him wait for my answer as I swirl my tongue around the head of his cock.

"I did. They know I'm here right now, and they know I might stay the night." I rest on my heels and look up at him, hopeful. "That is, if you want me."

With a growl, he hauls me to my feet and pushes me backward into the nearest wall. In an instant, he has both of my wrists pinned above my head with one hand. He's grinding his hips against me, while his face is inches from mine. There's a rush of dampness between my legs as his eyes smolder with lust.

His voice is husky now. "I want you."

When he claims my mouth, plunging his tongue inside, I moan. The ache in my core becomes more insistent. I twist, trying to free my arms, but he's gripping them tightly.

He breaks the kiss off. "I love you, Eve. And if you want me, I'll worship you for the rest of our lives."

There's a fluttering in my chest, like a swarm of butterflies beating their wings, trying to escape. This is so much more than sex, or even training, or an arrangement. Are we crazy? How can we have fallen in love so fast?

When his grasp on my wrists ease, I free my hands and slide

them around his neck. I don't know how we fell so fast, but it doesn't matter. He's the one for me.

I stand on my tiptoes and whisper in his ear. "I love you, too."

My words drive him crazy, and he thrusts his cock against the lace of my panties, moaning in frustration when they block him from fucking me. He makes quick work of removing my bra as I arch against him, urging him on.

Once my breasts are free, he dips his head down and captures a nipple between his teeth, flicking his tongue against it. Shivers of pleasure and pain ripple through my body and straight to my pussy.

God, he needs to fuck me.

While his tongue is busy, his hands are as well, and when he reaches down to rip the crotch of my panties, exposing me, I gasp with delight.

He lifts one of my legs, angling me just right, and when the thick head of his cock presses against my entrance, a loud moan rips from my throat. In one hard thrust, he drives his full length inside me, and I cry out, clinging to him as my other leg hooks instinctively around his waist. The intensity, the fullness—it's everything I've been craving. He's everything I've been craving.

He grips my ass, digging his fingers into me as he easily holds me, sliding his length out until just the tip is still inside me, then drops me down on his cock again.

"Yes. God, yes!" I cry as he bottoms out.

He pumps his hips, bouncing me on his cock. The friction is incredible and sends a cascade of delight through my body. Every nerve is alive and singing. Every inch of my skin is electrified, and the pleasure is so intense, it's almost painful.

When he moves his other hand down to rub my clit, the combined sensations are too much. I scream his name as I explode, convulsing with a powerful orgasm. My vision flashes, leaving me breathless and boneless.

When he grunts, I hold him tighter, not wanting him to stop

or ever let go. After a few more pumps of his hips, he presses my back against the wall as he empties himself, pulsing his release.

I clutch his shoulders, enjoying the warmth spreading through me from where our bodies are connected.

When Derek lifts his head to give me a slow, gentle kiss, I know that we've come a long way, and we'll go even further together.

When the kiss ends, I whisper, "Thank you for training me."

With a chuckle, Derek kisses the tip of my nose and carries me to the bedroom. "Oh, baby girl, the training just started."

"Promise?"

His reply is soft. "I promise."

He sets me on the bed and gives me a tender, lingering kiss. "I love you."

There's so much emotion packed into his simple statement, and he could tell me he loves me every day for the rest of my life and I'd be happy. I want to shout my love for him and never leave his side.

I reach up and touch his cheek, marveling at how his expression lights up at my touch. "I love you too."

He pushes me back on the bed, and this time when he slides in, it's tender and loving. He draws it out, bringing me to the brink and then pausing repeatedly, until when we finally orgasm together, we're shaking from the intensity.

My brain is mush once we've finished, and we cuddle up. The only sounds are the furnace and the rhythmic beat of his heart against my ear. I have no regrets. I've found everything that I've ever dreamed of, and then some, and now I'm going to hold him close and never let him go.

This wasn't what either of us expected, but sometimes the most wonderful things are a surprise. I know without a doubt that he's mine, and I'm his.

For all time.

CHAPTER 22
Epilogue – Eve

When I wake, Derek is spooning me, his hand cupping my breast like he owns it. Like he owns *me*.

His palm slides down over my stomach, resting on the small swell of my belly. His thumb strokes across the barely-there bump, so tender and possessive it makes my chest ache. Even half-asleep, he knows exactly where to touch, like he's staking his claim all over again.

His cock hardens against my backside, sliding low to tease my folds. Heat sparks in my body, and I'm already aching for him.

His fingers circle my nipple, lazy and slow. I'm soaked and my pussy throbs with need.

"Do you want Daddy to fuck you?" he murmurs against my ear, sounding rough from sleep.

"Please," I whimper.

He chuckles and presses into me in one long, deep thrust that makes me cry out in pleasure. This is my life now. We've been living together for three months. I work at his shop, helping customers, and sneak into his office for punishment whenever I'm feeling bratty. And now? Now, we're starting a family.

I rub my belly. It's still early. Barely visible. But the bump is there. Real. His baby is growing inside me.

Derek covers my hand with his. "My perfect little breeding fucktoy," he rasps. His words send a fresh wave of heat rolling through me.

"I still can't believe it happened that first time," I whisper, breathless. "When we didn't use a condom…"

His cock twitches inside me. "I can," he growls. "I wanted it, even then. Wanted to fill you up. Breed you. Make you mine forever."

A shiver tears through me. God, I remember it too well—the wild, desperate way he took me, no barrier between us, nothing but heat and recklessness. And now, I wear his collar around my neck and have proof of his desire growing in my belly.

"You did," I breathe. "You made me yours."

"Damn right I did."

Derek pulls out, flips me onto my back, and drives into me again, claiming me with the relentless force of his cock and the searing heat of his kiss. I wrap myself around him, desperate for more.

His fingers find my clit—each stroke exactly the right pressure.

"More," I gasp.

"Greedy little thing." His gaze drops to my belly, where his eyes intensify with a heat that steals my breath. "You're already so full for me, baby girl."

The way he says it sends my pulse skyrocketing.

"But..," he adds, his fingers teasing slow circles over my clit, "we have something to talk about."

"Now?" I whine, rocking my hips against him

"Now," he says firmly and pauses his strokes, but stays buried deep inside me. One hand presses against my belly, like he can't bring himself to let go. "I've been thinking. About you. About us."

My breath catches, hope flaring to life inside me. "About what?"

His eyes lock onto mine. "Marry me."

The words hit like a lightning strike, cracking something wide open inside me.

I blink up at him as my heart lurches. I wanted this. I dreamed about this. Even though I've been his sub for months, even though we're already committed in every way that matters, marriage feels different. With his child growing inside me, it feels inevitable—like fate pulling the final knot tight around us.

He leans in, brushing his lips over mine softly. "Say no, and nothing changes. Say yes…" His eyes burn with devotion. "Say yes, and you'll be mine completely. You and our baby."

I don't hesitate. "Yes," I whisper, trembling but certain.

His whole face lights up, the fierce joy in him impossible to miss. "Yeah?"

"Yes," I say again, stronger this time.

He laughs, overjoyed, and crashes his mouth down on mine. "You and our baby," he murmurs against my lips. "My whole fucking world."

Desire rushes through me, and I push on him. He rolls over so I can straddle his lap. I moan as I sink down on his cock.

"I need you," I breathe, clinging to him.

He grasps my hips like he's never letting go. "You have me."

"I mean it," I pant. "I want you. Now."

"Whatever you want, baby girl."

I rotate my hips, fucking him hard and fast.

"That's it," he rasps. "That's my good girl. Take what you want."

"Forever your good girl," I moan, grinding against him, chasing my pleasure.

His thumb finds my clit, and I gasp, moving faster as the pleasure builds in layers.

Right before I come, he topples me backwards and drives into me with desperation. I scream his name as I shatter. Spikes of delight ping up and down my body as I'm lost in ecstasy.

He follows, roaring as he spills into me, thrusting deep, fucking his cum back into me as my body trembles with aftershocks.

When we collapse together, he wraps his arms around me. His palm settles on my belly once more, like a brand of ownership.

"I love you," I whisper, completely blissed out.

"I love you too." His speech is rough with emotion. "You, our baby—my forever."

My heart's so full it feels like it might burst. I've got him. I've got *everything*.

Always and forever.

This is home.

CHAPTER 23
Epilogue - Derek

"I should be back in about a half hour." I sense Evie's anxiety over the time she's been away shopping.

"Babe, it's fine." I bounce on my toes, holding the bottom of our baby girl in one hand. "Cassidy and I are having an awesome bring-your-daughter-to-work day."

"I just didn't want you to disrupt your day," Evie sighs over the phone. "I'm ticked off that the sitter canceled."

"It's cool, babe. This is why I'm here. Things happen, and I've got it under control," I say, humming quietly to keep our three-month old baby snoozing against my chest. I'm in my office, pacing along the window overlooking the shop floor with her strapped around my torso. "Relax, babe. It's your day off. Do what you gotta do. Whenever you get back, will be fine. I have a bottle if she gets hungry."

I glance out the window and give Joel the finger because he's holding a tire against his chest, patting the bottom treads, miming me. He laughs, winks, and rolls the tire to the car on the lift. I don't mind the jibes because Cassidy fills a hole inside me I didn't know I'd had.

"Okay, I'll be as quick as possible," Evie says. "See you soon, love you."

"Love you, too." I slide the phone onto my desk when I hear the call drop.

Cassidy squirms in the sling, making a little fuss. I check the time, do a little dad math, and recall the noise she made right when Evie called. A little sniff confirms my suspicion.

I pull the blinds so the guys in the garage don't have more ammunition, then grab the baby bag and clear off the top of my desk. Cassidy whines and sniffles as I lay out the bag and remove the needed stuff.

Changing a diaper is easy! Sure, it can be messy, but keeping her happy doesn't take much. I make noises and faces at her while I do the deed, and she claps her hands at my foolishness.

After putting everything back in the baby bag, I swing her back against my chest and redo the straps to keep her warm body against mine. Then, I pull up the shutters and grab a bottle from the cooler tote clipped to the baby bag. It feels cold, so I take it to the breakroom and run some hot water over it until it's tepid.

With the bottle warm, I return to my office, close the door, and sit on the small sofa along the wall. Leaning against one arm, I slide Cassidy out of the sling and into my arms.

As she starts nursing, I hum a bit of Led Zeppelin's Kashmir. Her eyes close, and I relax. Carl handles things in the shop, and Joel runs the shop floor smoothly, I can take a little break. I let out a soft exhale and sink lower into the sofa, Cassidy snug in my arms.

"Oh, I need to get a picture of this."

Hearing Evie rouses me from my nap, and I jolt awake until I feel the weight of Cassidy on my chest, safely sleeping. She'd started rolling from her tummy to her back lately, so I've been a little more cautious when I put her down for a nap. I pat her back, reassuring myself she's safe.

"No, close your eyes again," Evie says while holding her phone to take a picture. "Nana Janice will love this one!"

I suppress a chuckle and resume the comfortable pose of cradling my daughter on my chest. I stir when Evie wraps her arms around my neck, her breasts pillowing behind my head.

She kisses me behind my ear, then nips it. "Seeing you like this makes me broody."

'Broody?" I laugh, then swing around to sit up. "Is that a good thing? You don't seem grumpy."

Evie looks at me and nods slowly. "No, I mean... broody, like, don't they say kids should come in pairs?"

"Is that so?" I say with a smirk.

"Uh huh," Evie slips beside me on the sofa. I lift my arm around her shoulder, and she leans into my side, staring at Cassidy, who is still asleep. "You know... she's sleeping through the night now...."

"And?"

"We can see if Nana would like to take her for a sleepover."

I snap awake, the thought of a night alone with Evie sparks a cascade of ideas. "So like a date night? Dinner, maybe a movie?"

Evie nods, pressing her lips together as she lifts her hand, tracing her fingers along my arm as she lays her head on my shoulder. "She told me she wants a little brother or sister."

"Your mom?"

"No, Cassidy." Evie punches my shoulder and laughs. "C'mon, seeing you being all tender makes me horny."

I glance down at Cassidy, then back to Evie. With a deep rumble I whisper, "You haven't been naughty, have you? You know better than playing with what's mine just because you're horny."

Her eyes flick up, and connect with mine before dropping to

watch her fingers twist her engagement ring. She glances back, biting her plump bottom lip. "Maybe?"

"I'm adding spanking to my list of things to do to you," I tighten my arm, squeezing her tight.

"Only a spanking? Pft. You don't love me anymore," she grins, her cheeks flushing. "I want more."

"You want me to breed you, too?"

Her eyes darken with lust, as she nods. "Yes, please. Put another baby in me." She kisses me, her hand dropping to my crotch, squeezing my stiffening bulge.

I groan pleasantly. "Call your mom," I say, standing and handing off Cassidy before I leave my office. "I'll tell Carl he's in charge."

The End

About the Authors

April Cross

Writer of spicy stories... okay, I'll be honest, most of my stuff is ghost pepper spicy. I started writing wife sharing stories before branching out to longer romantic erotica. I write power play stories with guys who demand to be in control.

Sign up for April's Newsletter:

https://books.april-cross.com/aprilcrossnewsletter

Find her books:

https://books.april-cross.com/

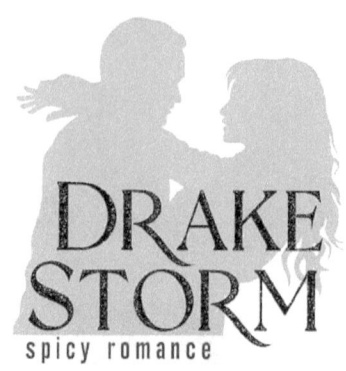

Drake Storm

Drake Storm writes spicy romance stories with all that you'd expect: a little bit of slow burn, spice on the page, angst, grand gestures, and a happy ever after (or at least a happy for now.) He lives in Texas with his wife, children, and dogs. He likes to grill, read, and think up stories that keep you warm all night, anxious to turn the pages.

Sign up for Drake's newsletter:

https://books.authordrakestorm.com/tempting-trysts

Find his books:

https://books.authordrakestorm.com/

Mating Lexi by April Cross

All I wanted was to find a guy and get knocked up. Now, I think I have found a soulmate. What?

Desperate times call for desperate measure—or that's what I keep telling myself on my hunt for a guy willing to take me raw and fill me up over and over again. Three years after losing my husband, I'm not ready for another relationship, but the clock is against me. I can't afford expensive fertility treatments, so I'm on the hunt for men who will give me what I need.

Until I met Noah.

His sculpted abs and gorgeous eyes ignite every nerve ending in my body. He makes me an indecent proposal—he'll fill me up on demand, as long as I agree to be his obedient toy. Am I willing to make this agreement to get what I want?

The way my body responds to him says that I will. There's something about him that makes my heart beat faster and turns me into one big puddle of lust and desperation. And when I drag him back to my apartment for a trial run, his dirty talk almost melts my panties off. After just one taste of what he's offering,

I'm willing to beg on command and do any filthy thing he demands.

Only, the more time I spend with him, the harder it is to remember this is just a dirty arrangement. Someone needs to tell my heart that we can't fall for a guy who isn't looking for a relationship and doesn't want to be a father.

I'm not sure how long I'm going to need him, but it's going to be one hell of a fantastic ride—and hopefully my heart is still intact at the end.

Note: This single POV novel is ghost pepper spicy with lots of dirty talk; including degradation. There is an element of using/manipulation as Lexi fumbles her way through trying to get what she wants.

Find it at:
https://stories.april-cross.com/lexi

Driven by Drake Storm

A Recipe For Disaster:

Take a violent Texas Thunderstorm, add a mistaken Uber, and mix in a jilted young woman and a jaded older man. Set the heat on high. Let them simmer through a road trip halfway across the country. What could happen?

Maddie: I'm at the top of the world after I aced my last college exam. I'm ready to slip into my fiancé's arms and get ready for our wedding. Everything comes to a halt, and I can't believe what I see and hear in my apartment. Full of murderous rage, I know I have to leave—NOW. I don't want to go to prison for a double homicide. I have my honeymoon money, so I can fly anywhere in the world if I can make it to the airport. My day goes from worse to horrible as a Texas thunderstorm soaks me to the bone as I wait for my Uber. I want to catch a break. Why can't something good happen to me?

Elliott: The divorce papers are signed, sealed, and delivered, and I'm ready to change scenery. I need to get out of Texas— NOW. I toss the last of my luggage into the back of my new black SUV and climb into the driver's seat. The sky erupts, and the storm clouds empty onto the roof of my car. That can't stop me, lights on, wipers on high, and head toward the highway. Slamming on the brakes, I swear at the figure who just stepped in front of my car. While catching my breath, the shadowy figure opens my door and slides into my back seat. I turn to give the idiot a piece of my mind, and words evaporate when I look into her eyes. Why can't I look away?

Struggling with the end of their relationships, thrust together by the circumstance of weather and too stubborn to admit their mistakes, Maddie and Elliott agree to team up for a drive to California. They can have spicy fun along the way, they don't have to commit, their agreement has a time limit, and it ends in California.

They need to get over their hurts and learn to trust again. Everything will be just fine.

Find it at:
https://books.authordrakestorm.com/driven

www.ingramcontent.com/pod-product-compliance
Lightning Source LLC
Chambersburg PA
CBHW051924240626
47153CB00004B/1349